ANTHONY SILMAN

MAX DEEPFAKE REVENGE

This edition first published in paperback by
Michael Terence Publishing in 2022
www.mtp.agency

Copyright © 2022 Anthony Silman

Anthony Silman has asserted the right to be identified as
the author of this work in accordance with the
Copyright, Designs and Patents Act 1988

ISBN 9781800944589

Cover images
Copyright © Belchonock
www.123rf.com

Cover design
Copyright © 2022 Michael Terence Publishing

Michael Terence
Publishing

Prologue

Life in Olderbury is acted out just as in any mid-sized market town in an English shire where cricket is played, Japanese and Chinese tourists photograph themselves taking photographs and German cars sit smugly and arrogantly, slightly distanced from the kerb. Lunches are sipped and politically correct conversations are confidently and virtuously spoken just loudly enough to be overheard at least two tables away.

The streets of Olderbury, pop 45,000, are lined with ornamental lime trees, equally spaced along smooth pavements. Its houses, a mix of new builds on new roads and Victorian or Edwardian villas and mansions on older roads, are uniformly well maintained. They have balloon-payment-due-soon leased SUVs parked along the street or on gravel drives behind gold-tipped black wrought iron gates.

Many older houses now have anachronistic, labour-saving plastic-framed replacement windows, kept clean by franchisee pure-water-system window cleaners. Some gardens have a gardener; many homes have house cleaners. It is important for owners to clean up before the house cleaner arrives, and it is essential for the gardener to be on show at school pick-up time; front gardens have a social commodity value.

Those lower in Olderbury's taxonomic rankings live in housing association homes along potholed and broken pavement slab streets with more lampposts than trees. They drive the vehicles sold on by the trade after the first owners have finished with them. The non-drivers walk, cycle, or use the grubby, expensive buses that are overcrowded at going-to-work time and run almost empty for the rest of it.

Younger fledglings rent flats, some of which are new, purpose-built units, and some are in previously grander houses now converted into margin-maximising apartments and studios.

They have communal halls and staircases that accommodate expensive bicycles and often baby buggies and prams. Satellite dishes peer at the sky from rooftops like pallid fibreglass sunflowers. Parking permits have value beyond money.

Olderbury has a pulse, a pace timed to the demands of the national and multi-national companies that supply most of the work and much of the non-tourist spend. These are variously professional firms, telecom companies and IT organisations, many of which pay big wages for even bigger personal commitments. Every so often, one of these goes pyrotechnically pop and by some form of accretion, a new business entity spins into being. HMRC is always fascinated by such a renaissance.

Its High Street and once vital, wealth-creating Market Square are now pedestrian areas with too few pedestrians except for sporadic troupes of tourists. Shops close down more often than they open up. Those that open are of the hairdresser, coffee and charity variety, with the occasional vape stockist or estate agent trying their luck.

A new retail park has sucked the life, the shoppers and the money away from the town centre. It has the same shops as every other retail park. If the High Street and Market Place struggle, apart from the exclusive antiques, arts and fashion tourist-bait shops, the retail park thrives and separates the high-earners from their wages with skill, guile and ease.

Olderbury pubs come in two types: one where the high earners and affluent silver-spenders go and the other where the drinkers and dealers feel more at home. Neither is welcome in the other's bars. Cocaine sold in the boozers shows up in traces in the loos and on the dining tables of the posher establishments.

Multi-culturalism in Olderbury is most appreciated when presented in the form of a restaurant. Indian in many flavours, Chinese, Italian and Caribbean are the mainstays with interloping Greek, Japanese and Thai-to-Vietnamese gastro experiences fighting for the gastronomic spend. America is represented by golden arches and fried chicken drive-throughs. These have queues of cars at all times of the day and night.

Fine-dining French and exclusive epicurean English places cater for new pretenders and old money with equal aloofness. The younger arrivistes eat vegan and drink New World. The greyer, older diners eat meat and sip 'Les Grands Vins' and XO cognacs. They acknowledge one another with equal amounts of superiority and condescension.

Prosperity is Olderbury's proudest possession. Everyone is well off, even those who dodge monthly debt with deft credit-card juggling skills manage to maintain an illusion of affluence. The poorer people wear a coat of invisibility draped over them by the townsfolk because penury and hardship may be common in cities but not in parochial market towns where, if it does exist at all, it is 'obviously their own fault.'

Olderbury's grander townspeople suspect there may be some illicit drug activity but are secretly sure that if there is dealing in substances like cocaine, ("I've heard it's rather fun darling") and marijuana ("Actually, I think it's skunk that's being sold now dear"), it will be by and for newcomers.

In the safety of the bowls club and the Hunt Bar, international drug lords are so far from life-as-we-know-it as to be impossible even to imagine; their snowy product isn't part of the fabric of our town.

Or is it?

1

"It's fifty notes to you, mate." Holding a small, clear bag of unidentifiable white powder, Kevin Taylor, known as Sniff, offered another deal to another customer. He thought of them as mugs, punters, wankers, but then he thought of most people in much the same way.

Wiry, almost emaciated, Sniff at forty-three years old, looked like he might have had the IQ of a pot plant but his ability to survive rivalled that of lice. Not quite reaching six feet, he had a slight stoop, a bandy roofer's gait, and a face that wouldn't pass unnoticed in an identity parade. He had a thin, horsehair-like wispy beard, a long, thin nose with attention-seeking, chasmal nostrils and pale blue, with a hint of red, eyes behind some snazzy gold-framed reading glasses bought from a petrol station.

Sniff didn't get his name from any substance-inhalation habit but from his childhood runny nose. He got very ratty about it. He was happy with a snorting allusion but teasing him about being a snotty kid would result in an ill-tempered rebuff.

Life seemed easy from the start to Sniff, who never recognised the value of scholarly endeavour. School had represented no great challenge as he was rarely there. His dad had 'buggered off' when he was seven years old, and his mum looked after him when she wasn't too busy looking after herself and her visiting gentlemen.

Denied the security and love of a family, Sniff quickly learned to trust nobody but himself, and, as he hadn't experienced it, he didn't understand compassion or empathy.

Sniff's core syllabus was truancy and shoplifting with added exercises in territorial bullying when tougher bodyguards safely supported him. Secondary school extended his key stage subjects to smoking, drinking and selling goods that he blackmailed other truants into stealing for him.

His survival instinct led him to learn only the maths he'd need in life. He also used the few chemistry lessons he attended, not as the teacher expected, to follow the syllabus, but to research various processes such as getting the opiate out of analgesics and the rudiments of how to make the closest thing to MDMA. He learned how to cook crack too, of course.

Sniff knew where he was going from an early age, and his self-styled education served him as well as any university or apprenticeship.

In those free wonder-days of the late 20th century, Sniff built a profitable business. Using his version of performance-related pay, he employed other blokes who stole for him, beat up any dissenter, and protected him from competition or attempted intrusion from any authority. Some of his blokes had useful proper jobs too. Chippies, sparkies, brickies, and mechanics, all brought in legitimate money and could break into anywhere and steal almost anything.

They all learned to manipulate social services with a blend of appropriated inadequacy and vague threat.

When Sniff first left his mum's semi, getting a council flat was just a matter of maximising his abject circumstances, some heavyweight pleading and a little implied intimidation. The social workers recognised potential trouble when they saw it and immediately selected the line of least resistance. It worked for both sides; the social security officers were free to pursue less-menacing targets, and Sniff got a flat of sorts to use as a dormitory, a safe house for mates and an HQ for Sniff Enterprises.

From his premises, he managed his blokes with threat and cunning, and Sniff Enterprises had money coming in from multiple sources. His income streams included selling stolen building materials, lots of smokes and booze, expanding into 'twok-ed', (taken without consent), Mercs, BMWs and Audis for cars-to-order. Add to all that a bit of protection skim, mainly from vulnerable small shopkeepers of any nationality, Sniff having no prejudices when income was involved, and life was sweet.

But cocaine was where the future lay for Sniff Enterprises and "stash for cash" became its mission statement.

The police were Sniff's unlikely allies. He was always more than ready to tell the police about any other criminals he could finger. For seemliness, he had been arrested twice, and the Crown Prosecution Service took him to magistrates' court once for selling stolen goods. Insufficient evidence ensured there was no case to answer, but meant that Sniff acquired the requisite aura of being a police victim and thereby deflect any accusations of being a snout.

When his privileged position was endangered, Sniff informed on one of his own blokes and passed on enough evidence for a guilty jail sentence to be handed down. This satisfied his police patrons and scared his other blokes so 'shitless' that their loyalty was beyond doubt.

The police allowed him what leeway they thought appropriate for activities they knew about. Sniff abused this latitude with admirable creativity.

Sniff did his police liaison remotely and avoided being anywhere near Olderbury's police station. He knew all too well how the nick worked, where the real power lay and who were the more conscientious and less malleable officers.

Olderbury police station had been built in the late 1960s. It was a purpose-built facility, equipped with cells, interview rooms, offices for senior officers, a canteen, and a service garage. It had easy access to the dual carriageway, which led to the motorways. Like all public buildings of that era, the station became careworn, tired and scruffy. Its decaying condition was ascribed by some to a shortage of funding, by others to a shortage of effort and by most to a combination of these factors. It had a strength of plus or minus 100 officers, about 2.5 police persons for every thousand citizens. Olderbury nick shared its regional HQ's administration, vehicle, training, and call centre facilities. It handled a little under 150 crimes a year, out of which violent crime and anti-social behaviour were the most popular, with over 80 reported incidents.

Only five drug offences were notified during the year. Although prosecutions were successful in each case, an Olderbury News editorial asked why so few incidents had been reported or investigated in a town where cocaine was known to be a rapidly growing problem. The editorial had been written at the instigation of the Chief Inspector, who had noticed local mutterings about a lack of police success in arresting known dealers. The Chief Inspector's logic was that the newspaper should have been asking more probing questions about evident police deficiencies, but because the editor preferred easily-sourced, good-news reporting, his paper had backed off. If a planted editorial brought the issue to a head, the Chief Inspector could then answer criticisms publicly in a bullish and typically bellicose way with the anticipated effect that drug dealing in Olderbury would cease to be a chattering topic.

The town council in Olderbury, much derided by the town's newcomers, was more like a school reunion than a legislative body. Most of the councillors had been educated from primary to school-leaving age at the same town schools, most were traders in the town, and all had a personal and usually avaricious agenda of their own. They knew wealth-creation when they saw it, and they saw it in every tourist coach that parked in the dedicated car park, white-line painted on an area that had previously been a kiddies' playground.

The tourists came for the history, the river, and the exclusive shops. They arrived, queued at the ATM, bought a coffee from the always handily-positioned Café-to-go Citroen van, shopped voraciously and left; in and out in next to no time like tourist terrorist strike forces, leaving only their money behind. The exclusive shops' unwritten policy was to have a two-tier pricing system that loaded the usual price by an extra 50% for coach trippers.

The councillors didn't approve of their newspaper carrying

stories about drugs; it wasn't good for Olderbury's welcoming image and reputation for safe, gentle hospitality. They told the editor that such negative imagery would result in curtailed advertising spending. The editor always capitulated except when the Chief Inspector was leaning on him. The editor hadn't known that the Chief Inspector had discussed his strategy for a drugs editorial with the mayor, who had agreed that critical gossip needed to be quelled.

The High Street traders who weren't councillors were increasingly worried about the town's evident laissez-faire attitude to its drug problem. Over a seven o'clock beer in the Hunt Bar, they talked about how someone should do something and were only slightly mollified by the latest Olderbury News 'drugs question' editorial. Some of them knew the reality better than others. Those with back yards and side-entrance alleyways to flats above saw the detritus from drug use every morning, and they knew it was getting worse.

Doctors in the Olderbury Family Health clinic were also aware of the growing problem. It had taken a while for the emerging pattern to be spotted. The GPs liked to work a part-time rota and filled gaps with locums, making continuity and trend identification less direct. Increases in liver blockages and lung irritation ailments with associated lower blood pressure were eventually noticed, and some tracking metrics were initiated. The GPs knew that these symptoms suggested inhalation of laundry detergent and talcum powder, which dealers frequently used to cut their cocaine.

Sniff, like all dealers, cut the cocaine he received with whatever he could get. Burgerman had a bulk meat tenderiser powder supplier, a product Sniff took in exchange for an extra wrap or two, but mainly he used cheap industrial bulk detergent and talc powders. They cost next to nothing and could easily triple, or more, the quantity of powder he could wrap for sale. He knew some dealers added to the cocaine experience by cutting it with more exotic additives such as fentanyl or heroin for speed-balling, but that was a step too far for Sniff. He stuck to his old favourites but might vary ingredients with baking soda, boric acid or even plaster-of-paris, depending on economy and availability.

Despite the shopkeepers' concerns, some traders chose to go rogue and cash in on the new business potential. These were a men's barber and Burgerman independent burger takeaway. Everyone thought the betting shop was suspect, but the bookie denied any allegations a bit too furiously.

Despite the newspaper article, Sniff knew that as long as he was alert and took precautions, he could carry on, as usual, supplying cocaine to the ever-increasing number who were spending freely and living up to their dealer's nickname. He and his blokes dealt remotely from the Sniff HQ flat in cars, on corners, and in each of the rogue premises. The barber used his added service as a sales promotion and allowed deals to happen on Mondays and Tuesdays with special offers on Saturday mornings before the TV footy. "Something for the weekend, sir?" wasn't a jaded old joke here, it was the phrase of choice to make possible buyers aware of their under-the-towel, illicit opportunity.

The barber was an easy reseller for Sniff to manage. He was happy with the business boost that selling drugs created, and Sniff 'lobbed him a weekly ton' from the takings for his troubles. The lure of drugs didn't attract the barber. He knew the cocaine was cut with God-knows-what and thought snorting it was on a par with Russian roulette played with more than one bullet. He was a whisky man, "you know where you are with a bottle of ten-year-old malt."

Burgerman was more avaricious, demanding a 20% commission. His burgers weren't all that good, and his regular trade was far too irregular to make a decent profit. Burgerman was lazy, scruffy and venal. His patties were the cheapest he could find and sometimes came from a man-in-a-van who got them from a mate who peddled the meat another mate couldn't sell in his shop. Sniff was the difference between a lean week and a fat profit. Sniff knew it, and Burgerman knew it. Meat tenderiser and cocaine soon became Burgerman's bread and butter.

The bookie didn't tolerate drugs publicly but had his own price, sufficiently high for him to overcome his principles: free coke. He had a very high tolerance for cocaine. It kept him going when stress threatened to engulf him. The more he snorted, the more his anxiety subsumed him. Sniff didn't mind this arrangement; he regarded it as 'seeding' and reckoned that the bookie would start to part with real money soon as his dependency deepened.

The dealership network also had a handful of commission-only salespeople who had routes to market in all the town's major corporate employers. If there were going to be cocaine users in Olderbury, they would buy it from Sniff one way or another. His penetration of the town via his rogue traders and throughout the businesses, pubs and restaurants was solid and growing. It meant he didn't have to recruit and manage youthful street sellers. It was not that Sniff had any moral objections to this Faginesque activity, he just 'couldn't be arsed.'

The only flaw in what looked like an established trade was the town's vox-pop. Sniff knew it, the police knew it, the town's councillors and traders knew it, and the newspaper editor knew it. "How is it," went the vox, "that we all know where coke is dealt, but no one seems to do anything about it?" Instead of quietening the voice of speculation, the strategic editorial had made it louder.

2

"Fifty quid, eh?" said the buyer to his dealer. "Cheers, Sniff. It was only forty pounds last time. Why's it gone up so much?"

"'Dun ask me chief, I only know what I have to pay for it. I add a bit for me, and that's what it comes to. Your choice innit?"

"Yeah, I'll have it. Here," the buyer handed over five new ten-pound notes straight from the ATM. "Do you realise this is more expensive than a gram of gold? Where does it come from anyway?"

"You joking me? All this ain't exactly legal, y'know, and we could both be nicked right now, so for sure, I ain't telling you anything you don't need to know. Just take the gear and fuck off, Ok? And you can't fuckin' snort gold, can you?"

The buyer mentally cancelled the 'thanks and good night' he had intended in favour of a look which he hoped said 'and you fuck off too' as he walked away towards his banana yellow M3 BMW.

Sniff's gaze followed him for a few seconds as he thought, tosser. Then he walked back the few hundred yards to his flat where his chief blokes, Lardy and Arfa, were having a skunk rollie and a drop of cloudy, head-spinningly potent scrumpy.

"That's ten wraps already, should crack a few grand tonight," he grinned, pleased with his almost pun. "Did you sort the bookie out, Lardy?"

"'Course I did. That fucker snorts it, though, dun he, he's on his third wrap already. I think he's losing the plot. Told him I'll be back in the morning to collect the dosh, but the thing is, Sniff, I think one of us should be at the bookie's more often, y'know, just to be sure he's not snortin' more than he's passing on to the punters. His money's been right so far, but I reckon he's doing light measures."

"Explain the facts of life to him, Lard, in a gentle sort of way, of course." Sniff's mouth turned down in his practised hardman smile. "Then whip a couple of his CCTV tapes, we'll copy 'em and put 'em back to keep his governors happy, and we'll spin through 'em to see if we can catch him at it."

"Ok. You coming out for a swift half, Sniff? Me and Arf thought we'd go round the boozers to see who's about. That arsehole from the trading estate is usually in The Bell on Tuesday, and he shifts gear to loads of his mates in those fuck-off glass offices where he works."

"How come he makes like the big executive when he's just a junky?" went on Lardy. "Still, five hundred quid is bloody good going. Anyway, we're off, see ya; if we're not in The Bell, we'll be in The Carps. 'Spect we'll see Tom-the-blood-van and that girlie-filth in there too. I wouldn't mind getting filthy with her in her copper's uniform; she could use her handcuffs an' all."

Sniff contorted his smile again. "Lay off her; you're too fucking lardy for her anyway. She's Ok and knows what's what. 'allo-allo' says he's sorted her out. Laters."

The blokes wandered out into the orange glow of night-time, and Sniff went to his bedroom for a quiet supper of whizz mixed into a mug of scrumpy, then a smoke and a bit of online porn.

By ten o'clock, feeling depressed, anxious and confused, he walked out of his flat and tried some fresh air. It seemed to work. His faculties slowly restored, and his libido began to throb away with a dull urge. As usual, he felt sick and coughed up some phlegm that he spat out on the pavement.

There's some thieving bastards around, he thought as he double-locked his front door and headed off, skipping The Bell, straight on to The Carps. Wonder if there are any girls out, he asked himself, never know yer luck. I could do with a 'fit bit'. Sniff was pleased with his wit. His amusement wavered when he saw that look-at-me yellow Beemer in the Carps car park. So, that tosser's here, he observed for the benefit of no one. Haven't seen him here before.

Sniff wandered in, straight to the bar where he ordered a pint of Stella. Lolling coolly against the bar, he affected his best man-about-town pose and peered at his fellow drinkers.

The Carps, once a thronging home for Olderbury's less honest and more physical citizens, was losing regulars at a death-knell rate. The pub didn't go in for the niceties of the hospitality business. Its food menu was 'yes' or 'no' to aged sandwiches, and its décor faded grime with tints of tobacco brown still lingering from the old days when smoking inside was not only permitted but expected. The toilets were disgusting, with an acrid smell of stale urine and defecated kebab, which clung to the olfactory senses like egg white to a cooking pan.

Eric and Peggy, landlord and his lady, didn't entertain today's fancy rubbish, which they jointly opined, was for wimps and tarts. They didn't tire themselves too much in achieving cleanliness and certainly didn't see any value in customer service or even a friendly welcome. But Eric and Peggy never asked nor answered any questions. If necessary for special occasions, their statutory CCTV could malfunction or be aimed at a point away from any activity not to be shared with the authorities.

Eric was in his mid-sixties and had an intellect of about the same numerical value. Previously a railway operative, one with a clipboard, hard hat and hi-viz kit, Eric knew how to be offensive without effort. He had an ingrained hatred of anyone who looked like they would have travelled first class. His dislike for anyone who might think themselves better than he would diminish if the subject of his enmity bought a bottle or two of off-sales champagne. He kept champagne because he and Peggy loved to drink it. It was their secret tipple, and they were terrified that anyone would discover their love of something so effete. Off-sales made the perfect cover story.

Peggy lived for Eric, who she thought was just the manliest of men, especially when he treated her rough after a bottle of Moet. What Eric said was not to be questioned, which suited both of them very well. Peggy didn't clean too much, didn't like the regulars very much, was an appalling cook and didn't offer much glamour to the pub, but she knew how to be discreet. For all the failings of The Carpenters Arms, its MI5 level of impenetrable confidentiality made it invaluable to those who needed such secrecy protection.

As was the Olderbury way, the police had a special relationship with Eric and Peggy just as they did with Sniff and his blokes.

DCI 'allo-allo' Clive Roberts and PC 'randy' Amanda Cotter were duty regulars. Their mission was to observe known miscreants in their habitat and report any intel to their sergeant. They were on the lookout for stolen goods, illegal gambling, illegal slavery – a big earner in the Eastern European community – pimping and whatever other scam-du-jour they could identify. As covert operatives, the two officers would have been less noticeable if dressed up as the front and rear end of a pantomime horse and their frequent presence in the pub amused the regulars no end.

When on watch at The Carps, 'allo-allo' accepted the occasional wrap or two from Sniff as an appreciation of his diligence in taking note of potential alibis for him and his blokes, should they be needed. Additional wraps were available for not noting the more obvious deals that happened most nights by the darts board and ensuring that strangers were profiled and identified as neither spies nor outside dealers. A bit like police work, really.

PC Amanda Cotter had a different role. Randy Mandy, I'm Mandy-fly me, put a man in Mandy; the innuendos and predictable puns were endless and were fuelled by PC Amanda's reputation of being a bit of a go-er. Her easy virtue reputation came from one of the policing pair's few arrests, where she had posed as a girl of availability, supposedly being pimped by an oleaginous old-school spiv regular, to a suspicious-looking non-regular whom she immediately nicked for attempting to pay for sexual services. Despite pleas of entrapment and with no evidence whatsoever, the lecherous non-regular was charged and given a hard time but eventually freed from custody with a warning. PC Amanda got half-a-collar to her name and a less-than-desirable reputation.

She was very aware of Sniff's activities and his relationships with her colleagues but had always refused any bribe of money or substance. As Sniff looked around, he saw PC Amanda and the tosser in the yellow BMW in close conversation and didn't like it one bit. Did the tosser, aka Dan the Man, know PC Amanda was a fed? If so, was he asking or telling? Sniff's paranoia was surging when Lardy and Arfa lurched through the narrow entrance from the street to the bar. They had had more than one drink, Sniff could tell.

"Ere you two, look at this," said a tightly voiced Sniff. "What's goin' on, eh? Don't like it. That Dan fella could be sticking his nose in, know what I mean?"

Lardy responded as Lardy habitually did. For him, thinking before acting wasn't an available option. Lardy, with Arfa in close attention, did his menacing butch walk towards the couple.

"Wass goin' on …s'ee givin' you trouble, love?"

PC Amanda was amused and annoyed by this interruption and showed her displeasure by answering, "Sod off, Lardy, this gentleman and me are just having a chat, and it's nothing to do with you, Ok?"

"Yeah? Wotcha talkin' 'bout then?"

PC Amanda and Dan ignored Lardy and his chum but Lardy wasn't taking being ignored as an answer. He clasped Dan by the shoulder and heaved it jerkily backwards and downwards. Dan hit the ground, his forehead connecting with a barstool rung on the way down. He stayed on the floor, holding his hand to his head.

PC Amanda, who hadn't told Dan that she was Police, grabbed 'allo-allo and ran out of the pub. Lardy and Arfa followed with the same haste but less speed.

Sniff said to Eric, "CCTV?"

Eric said, "'Course not."

Dan attempted to stand and found he was being helped up by Sniff, who asked him if he was Ok.

"Oh, it's you," replied Dan. "Christ, I'm glad you are here. You can be my witness, I've been assaulted."

"Witness to what?" asked Sniff, attempting his innocent, open look. "You just fell off yer bar stool. Pissed, I reckon. Time to go home and stop causing aggro."

"What are you saying? I was right here talking to that girl when your fat oppo and his halfwit mate attacked me! You must have seen it, and so must the landlord who was standing right by us."

"You're well out of order you are. You was on yer own, and there was nobody else here than what's here now, innit Eric?"

Eric nodded solemnly in the way of a man who isn't for arguing.

"See, so fuck off now before someone really does give you a little tap, know what I mean?" Sniff stared at Dan's pale, slightly bleeding face and knew he'd won.

"You alright mate?" came an unexpected enquiry from Tom Alderton, also known as Tom-the-blood-van, for his job as a paramedic.

After nearly five years as a qualified emergency medic, Tom was used to difficult and often violent calls. He had no qualms about placing himself between Dan and Sniff. His first and only instinct was to do what three years of training had imbued in him, to care for someone who might be in pain.

"No, you're Ok," replied Dan in an attempt at being dismissive. "Nothing to worry about, I'll be fine, thanks, more pissed off than hurt. Did you see what happened?"

"Sorry, I didn't see it at all. I was over by the window. I heard a bit of fuss but didn't see what happened exactly. I just saw you standing here with this fella," casting a sidelong look towards Sniff, "and thought I'd better check you out. It's what we paramedics do you know."

"Oh, are you? I didn't realise. Thanks anyway for offering, but I'll be fine. I think I'll report being attacked, and even if you didn't see me being assaulted, would you mind making a note that you've seen me here? My name is Dan Rackham, by the way."

"Yeah? Good luck with that, then. I don't reckon the local police will break into a sweat following up on any complaint you make, but I suppose it's worth a go. I won't be able to be a witness on any medical or professional basis because I haven't given you a proper examination, but I am here, and I have seen you and I can – and will if you want – confirm that you received superficial injuries in this pub, if that's any help?"

Grateful for an almost-ally, Dan smiled and nodded his acceptance and thanks to Tom, who was picking up his bag and making to leave. Dan walked from the pub and to his car. Sniff walked back to his pint and Eric phoned the CCTV company to complain that his system had gone down again.

3

Dan Rackham, 37 and single, was a career man who believed in rewarding himself for his successes. He had a Master's in Computer Science at UCL and, after taking part in the Business Scholars Programme, a Master's in Information Science from Ohio State University.

He joined Onetelcall nine years ago after meeting the CEO, Spray Wilson, at a lecture in the company's hometown office in Medina, Ohio.

"We started here," said Spray at every available opportunity, "because Medina means 'City of the Prophet,' and believe me, we intend to make a profit!"

From a small start in designing high-security commerce systems, Spray's business had grown with every terrorist attack, civil disturbance, act of sabotage, hack and malicious system outage. He created a one-call business that assured its customers of an incomparably high level of safety and security in every aspect of their tech, all controlled and synchronised from a one-call point of responsibility. No one had to make any calls anymore; the system did it all as a fully-enveloping shield, protecting all systems in the client company.

From its offices in Medina, Onetelcall evolved into a multi-national enterprise in just five hard, glorious years. It built a factory half an hour away in Cleveland and opened regional offices in Olderbury UK, Strasbourg, France and Dordrecht, Holland. Onetelcall achieved much of its unique, built-in security by designing and manufacturing its own products. Each sale triggered a programme of analysis, scoping, design, feasibility, prototyping, testing, proof and manufacture. Very expensive but very dependable, Onetelcall even made its own chips in a hermetically sealed production unit. Each chip cost a lot more than a mass-produced example but the price brought not only just the best in quality but also the incalculable value of 99.99% impregnability.

Dan and Spray had talked for hours after their first meeting. They had a common 'ones-and-zeros' code of expression, and Spray knew that he had found the key person he had been looking for. Dan was trained in the methods and technologies of Onetelcall and when the company was ready, Spray and Dan jointly set up the European territory finding the Strasbourg and Dordrecht facilities together. With the essential personnel they had jointly recruited in place, they made the company successful throughout the EU and opened up new territories.

Spray made himself president and CEO of the entire company and appointed Dan as Chief Operating Officer, with full responsibility for Europe, the UK and emerging territories. Dan knew Spray's story and it filled him with admiration and ambition.

Originally just Ray, Spray had wanted to be known as Maverick but settled for the Spray nickname as it sounded like he might be a pilot in the powerboat racing he loved so much. In fact, 'Spray' came from Ray's first 11-year-old part-time job as a helper at the Cleveland Browns football club, where he was responsible for applying Tack Spray to the footballs. No footballer, Spray soon moved on to more fascinating interests such as computers, but his time on the periphery of a pro sport instilled in him the motivation of competition and worked-for excellence.

He achieved a Master's in Computer Science from the University of Stuttgart and an MSc in Advanced Cybersecurity from King College, London, which Spray did online while working for a doctorate in Cybersecurity at MIT.

"It is a global issue," reasoned Spray. "So, international learning is an obvious benefit."

He garnered valuable relationships with industry giants like CISCO, IBM, Sophos, and Palo Alto Networks through his universities.

For a couple of years, Spray honed his skills by working for DueDilig Security in Temple, London. Here he found a whole new education and quickly saw why the hackers were always ahead of the corporates. When he worked in the shadows, he discovered the tricks used back in the days of the early hacking groups like Cult of the Dead Cow.

DueDilig made its sales by knocking on the doors of the world's largest companies and showing them sample printouts of their most sensitive data. You soon get well-known and sought after with that sort of calling card, and Spray built his reputation. But it wasn't enough, and Spray knew that as control-by-chip moved into every aspect of companies from their trucks to their offices, their systems, from R&D to the shop floor and even their HVAC, in fact, any open port, then the demand for his evolved, integrated security services would continue to grow.

In the early days, Spray spurned the campus-style environment of Silicon Valley and chose to build his international empire in Ohio. It made sense. There was a big pool of talent to trawl for staff and a tempting range of prospects, including some of the world's largest and, therefore, most vulnerable big-brand manufacturers and retailers. Now a USA and European force to be reckoned with, Onetelcall was fulfilling its promise of rewarding massively hard work with a small, growing fortune for Spray and unbeatable remuneration with added job satisfaction for Dan. With some justification, Dan saw himself as 'The Man' with a long, happy future. He wasn't about to be floored by the likes of Sniff's idiot mates.

First thing the next morning, Dan called Spray to tell him some drug-dealing thugs had assaulted him.

"I have a feeling that coke consumption is on the up here, and I wanted to find out just how easy it is to buy a wrap or two, and that's how I met this prat Sniff and his henchmen."

"Go to the feds, Dan," was Spray's instant response. "Don't even worry about the coke. If you don't mention it, I'll bet your dealer and his bums won't. Why should they? But thanks for telling me, I appreciate your honesty, and, as you know, I don't think a little snort does anyone any harm from time to time. But if word gets around your town that you've let a couple of hoodlums get the better of you, well, that's not so good. You gotta be seen as being in control, Dan, that's what we do."

Dan thought about his boss's advice. They were more than employer and employee, they were buccaneers, co-conspirators and a tight fighting pair taking on the world. Dan didn't altogether share Spray's easy-going attitude to narcotics and was convinced that cocaine was infiltrating his Olderbury business. He wanted to know more about where it was coming from and how big a problem it was becoming. He knew that the odious Sniff was the shop counter but who was the wholesaler? He had planned to become a customer, and befriending Sniff was step one in his gum-shoeing endeavour. It wasn't working well so far, he admitted to himself with an inner grin and, knowing that he was about to sour even further his relationship with Sniff, Dan set off for Olderbury police station.

Why do I always feel guilty when I drive to a police station, he wondered, pulling up outside the 1960's carbuncle. He parked his colourful BMW in the visitors' car park. It's like seeing a police car in your mirror even when you haven't broken the law, you immediately drive like you are taking your test or have had five pints.

Unable to force a subordinate into the role, Sergeant Peter Hamilton made a rare appearance at the front desk when Dan strolled in. Sgt Pete took an immediate dislike to the man walking toward him. Dan was wearing confidence as fittingly as he wore his eco-friendly Italian handmade suit and English handmade brogues. Sgt Pete also noted the leary yellow £50k BMW. His immediate reaction was a desire to yell, fuck off, toff! He purposely walked away from the counter into the back office, thinking I'll make the dickhead wait.

Dan could read the situation like a short story as he noticed the desk sergeant's insolent behaviour. He strode up to the counter in his best peremptory manner, and although he could walk into any board room and not feel intimidated, Dan suddenly felt a reluctance to ring the 'press here for service' counter bell. But ring it he did and waited and waited. He rang it again with the assertiveness that comes with rising anger and waited a little longer. He was just about to go for the long, insistent press with vocal accompaniment when Sgt Pete meandered, with deliberate unhurriedness, from his inner lair.

"Good morning, Sir." Let's not give him too much.

"Yes, good morning. I've come here to report an assault. Can I see a senior officer, please?"

If Sgt Pete had negative thoughts about Dan before this opening salvo, he wholeheartedly wanted to kill him and all his tribe now. Senior officer indeed!

"Perhaps I'll do for now, Sir, and we'll see how it goes. An assault, you say, yeah?"

"Yes, an assault. Last night in The Carpenters Arms. See? Cuts to my face?"

"Oh yes, Sir, I see. Not too badly hurt then, are we, Sir?"

"I was physically attacked, battered to the ground and assaulted, and I want to report it. I want you to arrest the man who attacked me, the fat yob. OK?"

"I see, Sir. Shall we mind the language, Sir? We don't shame people in this police station by calling them names which insult their weight or education."

To Dan, Sgt Pete looked the least likely politically correct policeman he'd ever seen and knew that this was just the beginning of the obstruction and obfuscation he could and would deploy.

"Sorry, you're right, of course," said Dan, knowing when to mollify. "I'm just feeling a bit aggrieved and cross this morning, as I expect you'll understand."

"Oh, I do understand, Sir, we all say things we don't mean

sometimes. So, what I'll do is give you an incident report form, and if you can fill it in for me, I'll take it from there."

Dan took the printed forms, still battling his urge to berate the police officer for his lofty condescension.

"That's it, Sir," added Sgt Pete. "There's a table and chair over there," pointing to a classroom-like fitment in the corner of the entrance area. "I expect you've got a nice pen, but there should be a biro tied to the wall. If you haven't."

Dan walked to the desk unit as Sgt Pete retreated to his back office feeling slightly smug. Won that one, I reckon, he said to himself.

Dan took his time to write legibly, succinctly and accurately. He noted the event exactly, from talking to a girl he knew as Mandy to being attacked by a man called Lardy, whom he believed to be a friend of a man named Sniff, and ended with his conversation with a man he knew as Tom, a paramedic.

Dan had to ring the bell again to attract the attention of Sgt Pete, who eventually sauntered back to the counter and held out his hand for the completed form.

"Thank you, Sir. I'll take that now. Have you provided your name, address and phone number for me?"

"Yes, it's all there on the form. What happens now?"

"Well, Sir, I'll look at your case later and then the duty inspector will decide whether it warrants any further investigation. He'll decide if there may be cause for further action in the matter by talking to a person or persons you mention in your statement."

"Oh, I see. Well, I suppose I'll leave it with you then for now. You will keep me informed, won't you and let me know when you're going to take some action?"

"If it is decided that action is required, I'll be sure to call you, Sir. We are very busy with serious crimes at this moment in time, Sir, and we don't have the resources or budget we need for action in every case but be assured we'll do what we can."

"Ok, sergeant. Do you have to give me a crime number? It might not be a serious crime in the scheme of things, but it is very serious to me."

"Yes, sir, I can see that. As I say, I'll be in touch." Sgt Pete could be dismissive when he wanted to be.

Dan smiled his insincere thanks at Sgt Pete and escaped Olderbury Police Station with an odd feeling of being reprieved. He was also depressingly aware that Britain's finest were about to give him a demonstration of inertia and that if he was going to get any investigation at all, he'd have to push a lot harder. He wasn't aware of being watched.

Back in his car, Dan called Spray again.

"Well, I went to the police, but they don't want to know; too much trouble for them, and I'm clearly not worth the effort. All they could say was how busy they are with serious crimes, and the desk sergeant chap – and a real old-school belligerent bobby he is too – made it obvious that the crime against me just isn't serious at all."

"Ok, Dan," replied Spray, sipping his early morning coffee in the sunrise glow of his Medina, Ohio flat, "are you going to keep on their case or what? I think you should. We have an image to keep going, you know, and you can't let some jerk fed screw you about."

"Oh yes, Spray, I'm not letting it drop; there's too much at stake now. You know, I'm pretty sure there's a lot of coke finding its way into the organisation here, and I'm also pretty sure that that chap who hit me, one of the local dealer's chums, had a bigger reason for trying to frighten me than might meet the eye."

"You figure this dealer guy knows you're onto him and that you're gonna try to, what shall we say, curtail his activities?"

"I'm not sure, but it seems possible. Trouble is, old chap, I'm not sure what to do next. If I confront the dealer, I'll probably end up beaten up in a ditch or worse; if I chase the police too hard, I'll have to show my hand, and I'm not ready for that yet. My gut feeling is I might not have to do anything. I think they'll have another go at me, and when they do, I'll let you know."

"Cool, Dan, keep me in the loop and just say if you want me to do anything. I may fly over to the UK soon anyway. We've got a lot of planning to do if we are going to extend our EMEA stake. Don't take your eye off it, Dan, do what you gotta do, but the company comes first, just like always, eh? Hang loose old bud," Spray rang off.

Nearly lunchtime, thought Dan. Back to the office or time for a spot of tiffin? He picked up his phone and called Jo, his occasional go-to special projects organiser and his very-often lover.

"Got that afternoon delight feeling, how about you?"

"Ah-ha," smiled Jo. "Not got much on, so to speak, so could be tempted. Give me an hour. Oh, and you do the shopping, Ok?"

"Brill, Jo, consider temptation on its way. Bubbly and some finger food sound Ok?"

"Oh yes, that sounds scruuummmy, possibly a bit suggestive but mmmmm, Ok."

Dan bought two bottles of Pol Roger, some sushi, prawns in a Marie-rose sauce, sourdough bread, a mixed salad tray, some cold mini-sausages and little two-bite pork pies. He added some very sugary doughnuts, which he was assured were fresh.

Forty-five minutes later, he parked a few spaces down the road from Jo's front door. He sat in silence, partly with growing anticipation of the afternoon of lust and laughter that lay ahead and partly with a growing feeling of disquiet as he assessed, dispassionately for the first time since it happened, the events in the pub and his conversations with Spray. He seems a bit too loose about coke in the company, thought Dan, also for the first time, a thought he dismissed as soon as it crossed his mind, almost.

He didn't notice the car pull in a few spaces back up the road from him. It was the same car that he hadn't seen at the police station.

4

Jo - Joanne Hadge - didn't talk much about her past. She had a brother and sister she seldom saw, and both her parents were dead. They hadn't been a wealthy family, nor had they been close. Jo and her siblings had been brought up to be self-reliant, self-determined and self-assured. Her father had believed that the world owes no one a living and that what others had, they had. If you didn't have what they had, it wasn't their fault; it wasn't anyone's fault but your own.

"Don't complain, don't moan, just make it happen for yourself," he'd say when pressed for a little paternal aid. It seemed hard at the time, but Jo, now 38 and separated from her erstwhile partner, Charles, had made it for herself.

After several years of working in big-co marketing and promotional departments, she left her last full-time job as a conference events coordinator for Raglan Inc, a major IT consultancy, to go it alone as a freelance events organiser. Jo didn't do the typical corporate days and sales training sessions; she had progressed to creating exceptional, unique events for people who could afford them. For Dan, she had arranged, for his selected potential customers to have as-inside-as-you'll-ever-get tours of GCHQ, one-to-one days with highly illicit hackers and some privileged experiences with the CyBOK boffins at the National Cyber Security Centre.

It had been at dinner at Lucknam Park, after a day at NCSC's MOD facility at Corsham, that Dan and Jo first interlocked ankles. Their sous-la-table affair quickly progressed to full-bodied fun in hotel rooms wherever their joint travels took them. Over the last two years, they had travelled a lot.

Jo, as a child, had been what used to be called a tomboy before it had any transexual implications and described the sort of young girl who had the bravery and inquisitive exploratory instinct that is usually associated with older boys. She also romped through her later teen years with what she described as 'a rather male attitude to sex,' having troops of young buck followers enthralled by her striking good looks and her compelling combination of coquettishness and audacity. Quick-witted and naturally funny, Jo had reached maturity without losing any of her exciting, provocative essence.

She had been introduced to sexism and misogyny at work in an era before online outrage had exacerbated such attitudes. For Jo, it was a matter of amusement more than threat or intimidation at the time. She soon learned to recognise the sort of men who would be predators and who felt challenged by her confidence and mental agility. The weak, inadequate chauvinists were frequently of limited physical appeal; their success with women relied on their ability to bully or pull rank. They would stand too close in lifts and let their hands wander. Or they would squeeze into tight spaces in store cupboards or by the coffee point where she stood. They would pinch her bottom, stroke her thighs, and attempt even more repugnant personal invasions.

As a young rider, Jo had experienced a bolting horse and found, by accident, that urging the horse to go faster, rather than trying to haul it to a halt, so confused the headstrong animal that it stopped galloping. The same technique, she found, worked with these mentally impotent men.

"Where shall we go for the weekend?" was often enough to deter the most breathless married man, while "let's see how big it really is" would usually result in a less than manly retreat. Jo enjoyed the game; most of all, she relished tormenting the deficient, ineffectual managers who strove to enhance their careers by claiming credit for her ideas.

"I'm not being insulted by a guy who sits down to pee," was just one shot from her arsenal of withering retorts. The deriding belittlements worked, and Jo's reputation as a girl not to be messed with reached iconic levels. She was an inspiration for many other younger girls in the company.

Whilst Jo's working life was both entertaining and rewarding, married life hadn't been all she'd hoped for. Charles had been a charming and sophisticated suitor and promised a secure, stable future. But as Jo flourished, Charles became more possessive, oddly jealous, surly and taciturn. His insecurities undermined his self-worth, firstly at work and then at home.

After separation and an easy divorce, Jo was as thrilled to find Dan as he had been to meet her, and their relationship grew impulsively to an exciting intensity. Although over two years had sped by since their first staying awake all night together, Dan still felt that frisson of aroused anticipation as he pushed the intercom buzzer by Jo's front door.

"Hope you've still got that lunchtime feeling," grinned Dan as he carried his shopping bags through Jo's first-floor front door. "I've got a proper picnic here and some bubbles too, of course. Glasses?"

Jo was going to take a couple of flutes from her posh-stuff cabinet but decided on two tumblers instead. "Here, splosh it in Danny-boy."

Dan did as he was asked. "Bottoms upwards, my lovely girl," he said, passing a glass of frothy champagne to Jo. "Here's to afternoons as they should be spent, in afternoon delight, as the Starland Vocal band once said."

"Up yours too chummy," smiled Jo as she sipped through the foam. "Oooh and sushi too, yum. Let's get nibbling."

Knowing that the afternoon stretched ahead with no demands and nothing else to worry about for a short, blissful time, Jo and Dan applied themselves to their lunch and their suggestive, playful chat. They enjoyed the sense of trust, belonging, excitement, and naughtiness they shared so closely.

Some considerable time later, as the sodium glow of the streetlight had supplanted the yellow warmth of the afternoon sun through Jo's sash windows, talk turned to Dan's pub fracas and his experience at the police station.

Looking down over the Olderbury shopping street below Jo's flat, Dan reflected, "You know this little town is going downhill at a rate of knots Jo. I know there's coke coming into work, and I know where it comes from. What I don't know is who the intermediary is between the dealer and my offices. I know it's an insider, at least I think I know, but I just don't know who, and now I've crossed swords with that Sniff dealer chappie and his oiks I'm not sure how to track down my coke-mole."

"Don't you think the police will do anything then?" Jo was leaning back against her favourite squishy cushion on the floor and looking at Dan with some concern. "If they don't investigate, I suppose you'll keep on digging until you get badly hurt. You probably got off lightly this time in the pub but next time it might be somewhere more isolated, more dangerous and then what?"

"I can look after myself, Jo." Dan had less confidence in his self-defence abilities than he wanted to show. "But no, I don't think the police will spring into any action at all. I got the feeling they didn't want to know."

"Look, I know some people who know some people who investigate things; you've met some of them with me. Would you like me to have a word and see if I can find a professional to look into your drug problem at work? Don't say no 'cos you think you won't be my hero anymore. Just accept that you are professional at what you do, and people who investigate drug dealers are professional at what they do. That's why people specialise. We shouldn't pretend we can do what we don't know how to do properly or safely come to that."

"Thanks, Jo, I'm not so wimpy as to worry about being a hero or not, and I know I'm no street-fighter, but for now, I think I'll just keep my eyes open and hope I can find something new which will help me track down just who is doing what."

Jo smiled in tacit agreement. "You know, I can understand alkies buying bottles of booze, there are very clever counterfeits and suspiciously cheap stuff which is probably anti-freeze, but generally, you know where you are with sealed, branded bottles, but, for the life of me, I don't know why people buy little bags of white powder when they have absolutely no idea what's in them. Completely bonkers I'd say."

"That reminds me," he said. "I've still got the bag I bought from Sniff. I'd better find somewhere good to hide it, or I suppose I could throw it away, but I'd quite like to have evidence."

"For God's sake, don't be walking about with dope in your pocket; the police would love that if they found it. Leave it here for now, and I'll hide it until we can think of something better."

"Yeah, that's a bit of a plan, thanks. Last thing I need is to be stopped and for the police to find some coke on me."

"Cool, hand it over, and no peeking; I'll hide it somewhere safe." She took the small poly bag and walked towards her kitchen. "I vaguely know your man Sniff, you know," she called across the room, "he used to come into the offices when I worked in-house at Raglan. Slimeball, if you ask me, I remember he came to the pub once when we were having a bit of a do and was a pest, wouldn't leave me alone and kept calling me Jo-Jo and 'Arizona grass,' Beatles reference obviously and he pissed me off to a very great extent I can tell you."

"Was he dealing in your old company do you think?" asked Dan.

"No idea what he was doing or why he was there, but I wouldn't be surprised, there was a lot of pot and skunk in the art department, and I suppose it had to come from somewhere. Horrible little man used to talk to the designers quite a lot, so it makes sense."

"Well, slimeball is right on the money as far as that man is concerned, he's getting under my skin, and I want to get him, I want him out of my building and out of the lives of my people, but I've no idea how I'm going to do that, and I'm sure the police aren't going to weigh in even if I can find evidence against him.

Bugger it."

"Are you staying tonight?" she asked. "We've still got some bubbles and food leftover, and I've got more wine and goodies in the 'fridge… and, well, I might be up for seconds if you think you can manage it?"

"Ha, I'm sure I might be up to the challenge. Put a tray together while you're there, and we'll have an early night."

Dan turned down the lights and smiled at the triteness of putting some gentle music on the player. He then walked over to the windows to pull down the blinds. He looked out over the quiet street below and gazed along the row of closed shops and parked cars. He didn't particularly notice the rusting old Ford or the man inside, looking straight at him.

5

Duggie Miller was inconsequential. He didn't even qualify for a nickname. He was just Duggie. He lived in a squat on his own, had no friends other than Sniff, and he wasn't too sure that Sniff was the good mate he claimed to be. Sniff only liked Duggie when Duggie could be useful. Duggie had a 20-year-old Ford Escort which still went and was still legal. He knew his car was his passport to continued friendship with Sniff and was happy to do the odd favour Sniff requested; usually delivering little packages, collecting little bundles and occasionally following people and making notes.

To prove his worth, Duggie had appeared in court when Sniff was part of a police action that had one of the Sniff-blokes put away. Duggie swore he had seen the bloke at an incriminating time in an incriminating place, and he was very believable, even though Duggie had never seen the bloke before he looked at him in the dock. He had enjoyed his moment in the spotlight; it was a highlight in a life that had been short on any sort of attention, even less of approval or praise.

At school, Duggie had been a loner. This wasn't a voluntary state, it was simply that he didn't fit in. He wasn't bullied, he didn't attract any attention at all. He wasn't even derided or ridiculed. He was in the background, towards the lower end of academic achievement and poor at sports. Duggie didn't even rank as a misfit. He seized on social media quickly and eagerly. If he couldn't be significant in real life, perhaps he could build a virtual persona of more interest. He had seen girls, lots of girls all beyond his reach, use Instagram to make people like them. Here was a way of creating friends and attracting 'likes.' He posted carefully crafted selfies and created a profile so cleverly that his old teachers would have been amazed. He became a new Duggie, a man with charisma, looks and sex appeal. Duggie almost touched a dream. Then he discovered what trolls could do.

His eyes stared at the comments. He didn't want to read them, but he couldn't look away. Perv, paedo, weirdo, shitstain, fuckface; who said names will never hurt me? thought Duggie as his self-worth plummeted from zero downwards. Memes, distortions and cartoons of his selfies began to proliferate over social media channels, and Duggie ran away. He tried to delete his accounts but found he was trapped in the virtual world where he had hoped to find salvation. He stopped looking, stopped posting and sank back into the safe comfort of invisibility.

When Sniff started talking to him, quite by chance, it seemed. Duggie felt he'd found a friend. Sniff was smiley and supportive; he told him he could see potential in Duggie and would like to give him a helping hand. He could put a bit of work Duggie's way to earn some decent money that social services and Universal Credits would never need to know about.

And Sniff had been as good as his word; it was something of a first in Duggie's life. Sniff had also treated Duggie to a little snort of 'something to make life a bit brighter.' When Lardy and Arfa took Duggie out for a pint or two and Sniff treated them to a curry, Duggie had arrived, he felt a sense of belonging for the first time in his life, and he'd do anything to keep it. 'Do anything' included sitting in his car for hours on end watching people. He was used to it. He had a flask, some pork pies, some country and western music CDs and the warm blanket feeling that doing something for his friends gave him.

"Yeah, Sniff. All right?" Duggie called Sniff from his on-watch stakeout. "He's stayin' with the posh girlie tonight seems to me. All the lights have been switched off, and nothin's happened for fuckin' ages, what ya say?"

"Fuck' sake, Dug, it's fuckin two in the morning. What you fuckin' calling me at this time for? Christ's sake, I was 'sleep."

"Sorry, Sniff, you said to keep you informed and wasn't going to drive off without tellin' you first in case you didn't want me to."

What a dickhead, thought Sniff. "You're alright Duggie, sorry mate, 'course you shoulda called me, s'Ok. He's a greedy fucker in' he? All afternoon and all night, I'll have some of what he's takin'."

Duggie chuckled. "Ok if I go home now, Sniff? I'll come back first thing, and if he ain't here, I'll catch him at his gaff or round his works."

"Yeah, go and get some kip now, Duggie, and don't worry about tailing the arsehole tomorrow, I know where he'll be. Have a day and come round the Carps later tonight, Ok?"

Duggie smiled to himself in delight. "Thanks, Sniff, mate. I'll do that. Great. See ya."

He didn't drive off straight away. Relaxing from his vigil, Duggie looked at his surroundings. The flat was an old building that had once been a fine home for someone important in the town. Like the other old houses in the street, the building had become shops with flats above. The exceptions to the shops-and-flats development were a pub on the corner opposite the tart's flat and a posh-ish 'Eyetie,' as Duggie described it, called, not that unusually, Trattoria Veneziana, which operated on all three floors of its very English townhouse.

Usually content in his comfortable, self-acknowledged mediocrity, Duggie's mind started to wonder about what might have been and what might yet be. Would he, one day, have a girlfriend, or a flat, or even be able to afford to eat at that the Eyetie? What did the man he was following do to give him so much? What, he wondered, was Sniff's interest in this man? He didn't look like a smackhead. He didn't look to be an idiot like so many of Sniff's customers. He looked Okay, and Duggie thought that if he couldn't be Sniff, he'd quite like to be like Dan-the-man.

Eventually, the old Ford tap-tappeted its way along the road and back to Duggie's squat by the station. It might be just a squat, but it was a clean squat. Duggie always kept himself clean and presentable. It was one of the few lessons which stuck with him from his memory-free, colourless childhood. He slept in a washable sleeping bag and had his daily meal on plates, which he fastidiously washed after eating.

After a good, day-long sleep and an evening shave, Duggie set off for his night with his friends and walked to the pub.

"Tell you what, Sniff," said Duggie, "she fuckin' tasty, that fella's tart."

"I'd give her several," joined in Lardy, whose opinion of his endless libido massively exceeded his ability, experience or opportunity.

"What ya got me followin' 'im for then?" Duggie had wanted to ask this for ages and now seemed like a good time to be more inquisitive than was usually allowed.

"I don't trust the fucker," answered Sniff. "These two know that," nodding at Arfa and Lardy, "and after we gave him a little tap here and he went to the rozzers, I don't like him even more."

Sniff didn't add that he thought the man, Dan, was on to him, that he thought Dan had posed as a customer to find out more about Sniff's activities. Sniff also didn't add that he felt an inexplicable, personal enmity for this man in particular. It could be jealousy, it could be fear of being found out, but it was very real, and Sniff itched to teach that Dan-the-man a lesson or two.

"Rozzers, yeah," said Arfa suddenly, "where's that girl filth tonight, eh? Now she's worth a fuckin' good seein' too."

"Like she'd be pantin' for your mini-dick," replied Lardy dismissively, ignorant of the irony.

Even Duggie smirked to himself. Duggie knew he was not one of the world's most desirable lovers, but even he found Lardy's and Arfa's crude self-delusion quite absurd.

"Who knows what she'd like," muttered Sniff, "they're all a fuckin mystery. Take that tart. I tried to talk to her at some fuck-off do she was at, didn't want to fuckin' know me. Cow. All chat-chat and smile-smile when we wuz wiv some of her chums and dried up like a witch's tit when we wuz on our own. Cow."

Sniff was silent for a while, looking into the middle distance.

"Wotcha thinkin' Sniff?" asked Lardy.

"Just thinkin' Lards, just thinkin.' Just thinkin' about the tart, p'raps she'd like me better if I let her know me more. Bugger it, get another round in Arf, I'll have a large voddy too."

At around 11.30, many rounds and 'voddies' later, even landlord Eric had had enough and told his best regulars to fuck off so he and Peggy could get to bed. With no shortage of ribaldry, Sniff and his little gang shuffled out of the pub and went their separate ways.

Sniff walked back into town via the park where, on a park bench, he treated himself to a little powdered self-medication. His demons wound him up about Dan and more especially about Dan's girlfriend who, if there was any justice at all, could and should be his and nobody else's. Now very drunk and doped, Sniff continued his walk back into town and wandered slowly past the pub on the corner towards the Trattoria Veneziana. He was truly pissed, in both the English and American sense of the term.

6

Jo's street-level front door, allowing access to an inner hall and stairs leading to her internal front door, was around a corner from the main street into a small residential road, opposite the pub car park. Sniff peered up at the dark windows to what he knew was her flat. He pictured her. He could 'see' her on her own, tripping about, looking sexy, being sexy. Addled and frustrated, he walked to and fro, along the main road, along the side street, past the pub on the corner and back again. He mooched and muttered to himself. Unconnected and unintelligible, random words such as cow, tart, fuck, tasty, fuck, tits and bitch crossed his mind as a familiar feeling grew in his loins.

"Bollocks," he cursed, "fuckin' have it."

Sniff saw his hand move and his finger pressed the bell to Jo's flat. He didn't move. Keep ringing, he thought, just keep ringing, she'll open up.

The sudden noise shocked Jo awake. Readily available via her work, Jo's bedroom benefitted from projection-grade blackout blinds and in the darkness, with the shrill, urgent noise attacking her ears, she was confused and perturbed.

Her doorbell unit, plugged into a kitchen socket, was in night mode and made not only a loud, intrusive alarm noise but also broadcast a high-intensity flashing white light. It seemed more like a corner of hell than her home.

What could be happening? Could someone be hurt and need help? Is someone trying to break in? Jo's thoughts collided with one another. Self-preservation had a say in this mix too. Jo reached out towards the sink's draining tray and seized whatever first came to hand. It was a knife, a sharp kitchen knife. She felt just a little safer.

In her loose bedroom wrap, Jo fought with her front door to get out and start down the stairs to the external front door.

"Who's there? Who is it? What's wrong? I'm coming! Are you Ok? Who is it?"

Jo lurched towards the sturdy old door and squinted her eye against the peephole. She couldn't see anyone.

"Who's there? Are you Ok? Hang on, just a mo."

Safety chain still in place, Jo opened the door and saw the slightly swaying Sniff, his unfocused eyes gawking at her.

"Help me, fuckin' help me," he pleaded.

Thinking he was either very drunk or very hurt, Jo's instincts veered from self-protection to giving help; she released the safety chain.

In a nanosecond, Sniff's boot was in the doorway with his full weight pushing, trying to force the door open against Jo's obstructing body.

Still perplexed, Jo said, "Are you hurt? Do you want help?"

"Tell you what I fuckin' want," snarled Sniff and Jo's inner alarm hit critical. She was being attacked; pain, even rape, were immediate real threats.

The contorted face of menace thrust ever closer, as the door inexorably opened. Jo catapulted herself, using the lower stair tread as leverage, at the front door, but Sniff's malodorous breath seemed to invade her nostrils and his malevolent face so close that she felt sick.

No hesitation now, yelled her psychobabble mind and Jo, knife in fist, launched a swinging punch at her attacker. For a moment, Sniff kept on getting closer, the door now fully open. Jo's terror reached maximum. She punched again. Eyes closed, fist tight, bowels churning, bile rising, sweat soaking her hair. There was another snarl, a loud, feral explosion of wrath. The foul face became smaller in Jo's vision, and the glow from the street darkened as Sniff's body filled the doorway, blundering backwards, his hand clutching the side of his neck.

"Cow, fuckin' cow bitch, you've fuckin' hurt me, you fuckin' slag!"

Now Jo was ice. Fear was becoming fury. She dropped the knife and threw another punch in one fluid movement. As her knuckles met Sniff's bony, prominent, protruding nose, she suddenly felt ridiculously delighted. Easy target, popped through her mind quite absurdly, and she grinned.

"Fuckin' laugh at me, you fuckin' bitch from fuckin' hell. I'll fuckin' have you for this, you fuckin' tart!"

Sniff's attack was turning into retreat, his yelling fading to moaning and his invective sounding more peeved playground than thuggish, violent street-talk. Staggering and stooping, he cleared the doorway, and Jo crashed it closed. The frame creaked as the door latch caught. Feeling a rush of safety, Jo chained the door and pushed the bolts, usually unused, into their catches.

Peeking through the peephole again, Jo couldn't see anyone or anything. She felt an increasingly desperate need to pee and felt a cold, trembling panic invade her body. Step by step, hand over hand on the bannister, she reached her inner front door. She didn't have time to close or lock it. The loo was a sanctuary, and relief flooded from her. She sat in this most private of rooms for she didn't know how long, and tried to visualise what had just happened, wanted to see it coldly and factually in her mind.

Cold and clammy, shaking and with a percussive headache, she lifted herself from the loo and made for the kitchen. Tea? Coffee? Brandy? She slid a nail, who cares if it breaks, under the tab of a can of fizzy orange and swallowed its chemical contents with a dribble and burp. The sugar started to work and her shaking subsided. Her headache, however, continued to clamp the nerves at the base of her neck and kick at her temples. With no idea how much time had passed since the attack, she called Dan.

"Oh Dan, I've been atta…." She could say no more; she could only let all the fear and anger express themselves in wracking, heart-wrenching wailing and sobbing.

Outside, on the street, Sniff was bleeding. He was angry, ashamed, hurting and confused. The dope had worn off and the booze was cooking its hangover in the pit of his gut. He hammered on the door of the pub on the corner. He knew it well, and he knew, dark though it looked, that it was still in the middle of one of its weekly lock-ins.

"Sod off, it's bloody half-past one, and no one's coming in here now," said a voice not to be messed with.

"Fuckin' open up, I'm hurt, I'm fuckin' bleedin'." Sniff waited a second for a response, and when none came, he shouted, "I've been fuckin' stabbed and I'm fuckin' dyin.' Open the bloody door! I need help, I fuckin' need fuckin' help!"

The door opened, it was Tom-the-blood-van, not the landlord, who let Sniff into the pub. Tom looked at Sniff and then inspected his neck.

"Christ, chap, just missed. You're lucky. Bleeding a lot, though. Sit down."

Tom Alderton was professional and proud of his commitment to his vocation. Even off duty and enjoying a lock-in, Tom was capable and functioning, if not entirely sober. He ran to his car to pick up his emergency bag. He also called for an ambulance.

Back in the pub, Sniff was telling anyone who'd listen or cared, few at that time of night, that the woman across the road had attacked him. All he'd done was knock on her door because he thought he heard shouting and, "What do you get? You get fuckin' stabbed, that's what."

Tom applied a temporary dressing, and by the time the ambulance arrived, much of Sniff's bombast had returned.

"She should be fuckin' locked up, murderous cow," he

declared. "Try to do an old mate a good turn and get turned on alright, stabbed in the fuckin' neck."

The ambulance men were unimpressed by Sniff's excessive outrage. The police arrived in the form of PC Thomas (known as John, of course) and PC Pitt (aka Brad). They were more impressed by Sniff's story and accepted without too much doubt that big man Sniff had been murderously and purposefully attacked by the petite woman in the flat across the road as he attempted to rush to her aid.

The ambulance took Sniff to hospital, where a quick and minor operation successfully dealt with a laceration just a tad away from his left common carotid artery. Sniff felt oddly heroic when he was told that a centimetre further left would have sent him to the great coca plantations in the sky.

The two PCs, sirens and blue lights on, rushed back to the nick to discuss the next urgent action to be taken with their sergeant.

Dan, hearing only a snippet of Jo's terrified and fragile state, urged his M3 to her flat faster than legal or safe and was with her before the police and ambulance arrived at the pub on the corner. He and Jo heard the emergency services below them and wondered what would happen next.

7

Jo's doorbell sounded in the night yet again. This time Dan opened the door to see two police officers, in regulation arms to the front stance, crowding the doorstep.

"Jo Hadge?"

"No, I'm Dan Rackham. I'm a friend of Jo's. She is terribly upset. She has been attacked on her own doorstep. That's why you are here?"

"Something like that, sir, we'll come in now, sir. Upstairs, is she?"

The two PCs, broad and solid in their heavy clothing, clambered up the stairs slowly and deliberately and stood in Jo's sitting room, both reaching for their notebooks. After introducing themselves in the prescribed way, PC Thomas took the lead and asked Jo to confirm her identity, age and, perhaps a little superficially, her address. She was then asked to describe, in her own words, just to ensure she didn't steal anyone else's words, what had happened that night and explain the circumstances that led to her stabbing the victim.

Aghast at the implications, Dan protested, "Jo is the victim here, officer. She has been attacked, threatened and terrified by a drunken thug who tried to barge in and hurt her, even rape her. So, let's get the facts right here, shall we?"

"No need to talk of rape, sir, there's no question of that, is there miss – er – madam? We'll identify who is the victim and who isn't. We just need to know the facts, and we need to hear them from this lady, not you, so we can decide what further action can be taken."

Dan felt the same powerlessness he had experienced at the police station when reporting his own incident. He made the same decision again and chose not to fight any further.

"Jo, just tell the officers as clearly as you can, if you feel up to it, exactly what happened."

Jo explored her inner discipline and refused to allow the police officers to see any signs of weakness. Forcing herself to feel composed, Jo sat slowly and carefully on her sofa, head up, legs crossed, and hands gripping each other in front of her. Readying herself to tell her story, she noticed the other police officer, PC Pitt, moving slowly toward the kitchen.

"What's he doing?"

"We have to look round your place miss, er, madam and collect anything we think might be used as evidence," said PC Thomas with regulation police intonation.

"Evidence? Evidence of what? He wasn't up here, he attacked me on the doorstep. What evidence do you think you'll find, for heavens' sake?"

"We'll do our job, miss, and my job now is to ask you questions while my colleague looks around, alright?"

"I suppose so," replied Jo. "Just get on and ask your questions."

"Yeah, yes, er miss. Let's get on then, shall we? Just ignore PC Pitt for now and, first off, tell me why you didn't call us. If you'd been attacked, then you would call the police straight away, wouldn't you?"

Jo looked directly at her interrogator: "Officer, I have just been attacked; there has just been a man trying to force his way into my home, probably into my body, all I wanted, all I could think about was getting my front door closed and being safe. I called Dan because I didn't actually think of calling anyone else. I wanted someone to hold me, I wanted someone safe, someone I know and trust, I simply didn't think of calling you; it just didn't occur to me."

"So, miss, you say you are the victim of an assault and an attempted break-in, but you say you don't think it's a police matter, is that right?"

"I'm saying, again, I was attacked, I was frightened, I was in a panic, and I wasn't thinking at all. I wanted Dan, not anyone but Dan to help me and be with me. I just didn't even think about the police, after all, the vile pig who tried to break in and assault me had gone. What would the police have been able to do anyway?"

"I think what the police could do is up to the police, madam. It does look very strange to us that you inflict a serious knife wound on another person and now find excuses why you didn't want to involve the police at the time."

"I didn't inflict, as you say; I only protected myself from attack...."

"Yes, miss, I think what my sergeant will want to know is if the real reason you didn't call the police is that you opened your door to a person who you then proceeded to stab almost fatally?"

"Good God, man," exploded Jo in exasperation, "I didn't just stab the bastard in cold blood. I just tried to fight off a man who was attacking me on my own doorstep at some unearthly time at night! What's so difficult for you to understand about that?"

"I didn't say you acted in cold blood madam, that's your description, and I have noted it. But I think the best thing now is if you could tell me exactly what happened, this will be your statement made, as it is right now, not under caution, although that might come depending on what you tell me. So, miss, from the very start if you would?"

PC Thomas readied his ballpoint for statement-taking and noted down, as faithfully as his slow handwriting speed would allow, Jo's blow-by-blow account of the attack from the doorbell all the way through to calling Dan after the attack. Dan sat with her, his hand resting on her shoulder in comfort and support while she told her story. He could feel his fury rising as her tale progressed from shock to terror. He looked at the policeman's struggle with dictation and wondered exactly where all this would lead. He knew that Jo would need legal help before the nightmare had passed.

Just as Jo was nearing the end of her account, PC Pitt appeared again, now holding her robe, a kitchen knife, her phone and laptop, and a small polybag of white powder.

"Shit," said Jo before she could stop it.

"Are these yours, miss?" asked PC Pitt, showing Jo each of the items he had collected one by one.

"Yes," said Jo, knowing she was probably looking more guilty than she would have liked.

"Is this the knife you used to stab the victim?" asked PC Pitt.

"What is this?" said Jo, a little more loudly than her self-control would have wanted. "Why does everyone keep saying that the arsehole who attacked me is the bloody victim? I'm the victim. Look at me. I'm in my own home. It's still bloody night-time. I didn't go out hunting this creep down, it was him who battered on my front door, it was him who tried to assault me, it was him I had to fight off, I'm the bloody victim!"

Jo was nearly sobbing with anger, frustration and the remnants of fear which still gnawed away in her gut.

"Yes, miss," said PC Pitt impassively, "that's as maybe, isn't it, not for me to say, I'm just gathering evidence. So, is this the knife you used, er, in the attack, and is this the robe you were wearing at the time?"

"Yes, yes, for Christ's sake."

"And this here," PC Pitt held up the polybag between his thumb and forefinger, "what's this then, eh? Is it what I think it is, madam? Is it cocaine? Is it? Have you been taking any substances tonight, miss? And remember I will be checking, so don't bother trying to lie."

Jo felt despair and exhaustion drain her will to fight anymore: "Take it, take it all, take your bloody tests, I don't care, I just don't bloody care."

"By rights, I should take you to the station now, miss. But seeing as how you are so upset, and I don't suppose you'll be going anywhere, will you, we'll leave it for now. Me and my colleague will make our reports and file your statement and all the evidence. Someone will be back in the morning, that's this morning, isn't it, to see where we go next, but I should warn you it is likely you'll be charged with aggravated GBH at least. Anyway, that's what I think is most likely. If you aren't here in the morning, you'll be in even bigger trouble than you are now, so take my advice, eh miss, er madam."

With a last accusatory look at the exhausted Jo, the two policemen left the flat. Dan held his precious Jo tightly as she slipped into sleep.

8

Dan didn't regard himself as a local businessman even though his company was a sizeable employer in Olderbury. He didn't enjoy the local business and breakfast clubs that contrived to achieve mini cartels under a pseudo-professional camouflage. Onetelcall didn't use any of the local legal firms, and Dan's town contacts for this new and unusual emergency were all too few. He didn't want to ask any of his colleagues for advice and didn't trust a word he read on social media, so he resorted to a very 20th-century resource and did a web search for the best criminal lawyers in Olderbury.

Hedges and Co, est. 1923, stood out, not for its website or the persuasiveness of its blurb, or its testimonials but because it fielded, amongst its small number of specialist lawyers, a solicitor and barrister team and described with evident pride, their record of success. A quick call, emphasising the seriousness and urgency of the matter, resulted in an appointment for midday the next day. It was the best they could offer, and Dan accepted it with relief.

On the morning after that fateful night, Dan let Jo sleep in until he'd made his call to the solicitors and also a few calls to his office to tell his assistants that he wouldn't be at work for a couple of days. He called Spray in Medina at 05.00 to catch him at midnight in Ohio time.

"I know it's midnight, Spray. Hope you're still up and about!"

"You know me, Dan, the night is for working and thinking. I'm just going through the spec for an installation for our tyre client. What can I do for you?"

Dan rushed through the headlines of the last night's attack on his much-loved Jo and told Spray that he'd need time to do whatever he had to do for her.

"Sure, bud," replied Spray, "thanks for telling me. You know you must take all the time you want, and if you need anything more from me or the company which might help out, well, it's yours, you know that."

After four and a half hours of phoning, emailing and texting, Dan had covered all essential outstanding business matters, and his mind willingly started to tangle with the looming crisis. He was making briefing notes in preparation for tomorrow's legal meeting when Jo's fingers ran along the back of his neck.

"Ok, darling?" he asked, closing his laptop lid.

"I think so. I keep trying to believe I've had one of those dreams which seem so real you don't know you're asleep until you wake up, but it isn't 'cos I'm awake now, and the dream hasn't gone away. Oh god, Dan, it's awful, isn't it?"

Dan put the kettle on and dropped some bread into the toaster slots. "Yes, mate, it is bloody awful, and those feds last night were completely unbelievable, weren't they? Talk about Britain's finest, it's no wonder the police are getting such a poor press these days."

Jo didn't think she'd be able to eat a thing, but some buttery toast smothered with deep orange marmalade tempted her to try a small slice, which, with some hot, strong coffee, soon became several slices and with it, an improvement in mood and demeanour. Dan ran through his plans. He told her about the solicitor firm he'd called and the appointment he'd made. Jo wasn't the sort who liked choices or arrangements being made for her and looked at him questioningly.

"Here's is the firm's website, here are the two chaps we'll see and if you don't like the look of them, I'll find some alternatives, of course, I will."

But Jo was happy and, under the circumstances, very grateful to be led for once.

"We've got from now until midday tomorrow to prepare our brief for the lawyers; I've just made a start, so now we can do it together if you feel up to it?"

"I'm Ok now, love; the toast seems to have fed my optimism, so let's get cracking."

Jo's optimism didn't live for long. A knock, knock, knock on the door announced the return of the police. Two different officers asked to be let in. This time there was a female officer, PC Amanda Cotter and the more senior Sergeant Mick Cowan. The sergeant took control and followed the procedures for which he had been trained. Sgt Mick had shared an interview strategy with PC Amanda in the car, and they had agreed that they should establish a rapport with the suspect but not consider either a fast track or a video interview.

"Jo, may I call you Jo? How are you feeling this morning? Are you ready for us to ask you some questions? Are you sure you don't need any medical advice before we start this interview?"

"I'm fine, really Sergeant, just go ahead and ask your questions, but I'd like Dan to stay with me if that's Ok?"

"Under the circumstances, Jo, we have no objection to Dan, may I call you Dan, sir, being present as long as he understands he is only an onlooker unless we have specific questions for him."

PC Amanda Cotter followed, "Jo, I know you have been through an awful time, and you must be worried and frightened. I am here if you need a more personal conversation or want to say anything you'd rather not say to a male officer. Is that Ok and all clear, Jo?"

Jo wanted to say, sod off, don't be condescending to me, but instead, smiled at PC Amanda. "Thank you, yes, I've had a terrible time and I still feel shaky but I'm happy to answer all your questions, let's get cracking, shall we?"

Sgt Mick picked it up again and surprised Jo and Dan with his first announcement, "We have had a conference at the station about this case and analysed your statement and the evidence taken from last night."

As Sgt Mick paused, Dan thought to himself sarcastically, he's waiting for the lights, camera, action call.

"I have been instructed to tell you that we shall not be pursuing charges against you in connection with you having a user quantity of a class A drug, namely cocaine. You do realise that if you'd had any larger, you'd be facing a big fine and up to seven years in prison, don't you? In your case now, my commanding officer has said he won't be pressing for the CPS to be involved with this matter. You're a lucky girl Jo."

"Thank you, sergeant, after last night, after being attacked and being terrified out of my wits, I'm not sure I feel all that lucky. I'm grateful that it's being dropped, but I thought I was going to have to take a test. Why has that changed, not that I want to be tested, of course?"

"I can't tell you any more about it, Jo, other than my seniors have told me that it isn't policy at the moment in Olderbury to consume valuable time and resources by getting the CPS to prosecute small offences like your cocaine possession."

"That's great then, sergeant, thank you. Can you tell me now what you are doing about catching the man who attacked me and bringing charges against him?"

"That's a different matter altogether, Jo, that's why PC Cotter is here, and I have to ask you some more questions. As it stands at the moment, our questions will be asked here in your home but will be under caution as I have been authorised to tell you that you will be charged, under section 18, with causing grievous bodily harm with intent. From your statement last night and the evidence we have seen, you deliberately selected a knife and used that weapon on the victim's head area. You deliberately planned to do that at the time you opened your front door. Is that clear, Jo? If it is clear, I shall now officially caution and charge you before we go on to the rest of our questioning?"

Sgt Cowan intoned the standard caution and handed a completed charge sheet to Jo.

"As you can see, a date has been set for your plea hearing at the magistrates' court. Your solicitors – you'd better get some representation – will prepare you for this. Until then, you will be required to present yourself at Olderbury police station on each Monday morning as a pre-court police bail condition, is that clear?"

Jo, pale and now shaking again, squeezed Dan's hand, desperate for human contact, some reassurance, something solid in her tumult of confusion.

"Hang in there, Jo, my darling," said Dan, "it's probably best to answer the sergeant's questions now and then we'll see what the lawyers say tomorrow."

"Got a brief already, eh sir? Probably very wise, it's a serious matter, and the CPS is sure to go all out for prosecution, I'd say. There's a bit of HQ action going on about stabbings and knife crime at the mo," said the sergeant.

"I'm not sure I understand your assessment here," said Dan. "The truth is that Jo was woken up in the middle of the night, had to fight off an attacker on her own doorstep and yet you say the attacker is actually the victim and that Jo is some sort of knife-wielding crazed psycho intent on stabbing anyone she can find, it's totally on its head isn't it?"

"Thank you, sir, I'll note your opinion, but the only important fact at the moment is that PC Cotter and I have a job to do, and that's now to ask questions under caution and report to our seniors. If there are any questions you'd like to ask miss, or if I haven't explained fully and clearly what is happening here, please say so now, otherwise, we shall progress with the questions which will start with asking why you didn't call the police as soon as the incident happened?"

Jo nodded to indicate her readiness. Dan, still clenching Jo's hand, used his free hand for note-taking as he anticipated a need for an accurate recording of her questioning session to relay to the solicitor. Sergeant Mick Cowan edged towards an armchair.

"May I?" he asked.

"Of course," said Jo.

The police officer lowered himself onto the unexpectedly low arm of the chair. "Ah ah-hem," in an amateur dramatic fashion Sgt Mick prepared himself for his inquisition. "First off, I must ask again, why you didn't call the police?" It was the beginning of rapid-fire probing. "If you were so frightened, why did you open the door? Why didn't you call your man here? Why did you choose a knife? Did you choose it because it was the sharpest knife? Didn't you look through your door's spyhole? Why open the door if you couldn't see who it was? How did the man try to attack you? Why didn't you slam the door in his face? Why did you feel the need to attack him? Did you aim for his neck? Did you know how dangerous a stab to the neck is? Did you know you'd hurt him? Did you see his blood? Why didn't you call for an ambulance? Why did you just ignore the fact that you'd stabbed someone? What did you do immediately after you slammed the door? Why didn't you call the emergency services after the incident...?"

The litany of questions flowed through Jo's mind in a riptide of confusion. She even felt a tinge of guilt at one point; had she aimed at his most vulnerable spot? But her answer came back loud and clear in her mind, I didn't aim, I just lashed out to protect myself with a lunge, not a stab, more like a punch.

She answered their questions truthfully and carefully and with each answer, with each vivid flashback, she felt the outrage of their doubting her innocence.

Sergeant Cowan reached the end of his interview strategy. He stood and shook slightly to re-arrange the fall of his trousers over his regulation boots. His shoulders squared, giving the impression of a man pleased with his performance. He moved to hand Jo his police document folder.

"Will you please read carefully through all of this? It's very important as it will be passed on to the CPS and it is all, as you know, made under caution and will be used in a court of law. If you are happy with what's written, please sign it at the bottom, just here."

The sergeant pointed to a dotted line. Jo read it, and for safety, Dan read it too. The sergeant had done a reasonable job. Jo signed.

"Good, Ok, that's that then, thank you, Jo, and thank you, sir. There will be a SOCO team here this morning too, they will need to inspect the doorstep and hallway and will also examine the pavement and road outside. You'll be here all morning, won't you? And don't forget you have to come to the station on Monday morning; failure to do so will be a breach of bail and probably result in a bail review and possible remand, Ok?"

Sgt Mick Cowan and PC Amanda Cotter left the flat but somehow, their presence lingered and Jo felt menaced. Coldness and anxiety now replaced shaking fear. How, she wondered, could her life have gone from wonderful to absolute disaster so quickly?' One minute happy, the next panicked and more afraid than she could remember ever being.

The now dreaded doorbell sounded its alarm again. Dan went down to open the front door. The two SOCO officers announced themselves and explained their purpose. Dan confirmed the location as being the site of the stabbing, to dispute the incident description would have been pointless. Dan asked the investigators to make sure they closed the front door when they had finished their work and went back up the staircase to be with his distressed, distraught lover.

9

Hedges & Co had been a beacon of rectitude and jurisprudence for nearly a century, originally the fiefdom of one Donald Hedges who had qualified at University College, London and trained with the Inns of Court. Possibly overqualified for provincial legal practice, Donald's reputation grew rapidly, as did his practice, and his purse.

Donald's son, Donald, not Donald junior as this would have been far too transatlantic, dutifully followed his father, although with slightly less impressive credentials. Nonetheless, Hedges and Co continued to prosper. It became the foremost firm in its region and built a team of some thirty lawyers working over the range of essential disciplines needed to service private and business clients in all their affairs.

It was Donald-the-third who, despite also being a highly qualified lawyer, saw the attraction of a world beyond his desk and the inner sanctums of the county courtrooms. He cashed in by selling the family jewel to a small consortium of solicitors led by their senior and most aggressive partner, Will Davies.

There was some prescience about Donald-the-third's bonanza exit. The close of the 20th century bought more complex and increasingly competitive times for the regional solicitor. Hedges & Co had become a sizeable group, it had amassed offices full of niche specialists, and the firm had become large, unwieldy and unmanageable. Will, a strategist without emotion or any need for continuity, asset-stripped the Hedges & Co corporate body, drove off unwanted consortium members and slimmed the firm to be exactly as he wanted it.

The new svelte Hedges & Co managed to maintain its established reputation while succeeding in pruning unnecessary weight. Employees and associates went, and the grand offices went too, rented out to a big company whilst Hedges relocated to an affordable and suitably Dickensian first-floor suite of rooms. The expense accounts went, the cars went, and Will had a keenly honed, specialist legal machine that he could control and that could demand and achieve premium fees for its efficient, uncompromising, and almost always successful services.

Will focused his business on just three sectors: divorce, motoring offences and criminal law. With limited overheads, assured legal aid fee income and high fees from wealthier, discerning clients, Hedges was everything Will wanted. It would keep him happy, fulfilled and very well off during his working life and more than adequately catered for in his still distant retirement.

Hoping that he'd picked the best available professional representation, Dan held Jo's hand protectively and reassuringly as they walked slowly from the street entrance, along the corridor to the lift that led to Hedges & Co reception area.

"Rackham and Hadge to see Mr Davies, please," said Dan to the blue-grey-haired woman who greeted them from the lift.

"Of course," she said with trim efficiency and a professional half-smile of welcome.

An unadorned, unvarnished finger waved at a dark brown faux-leather Chesterfield-style sofa on which Dan and Jo sat as implicitly requested.

The woman indicated a coffee pot and offered an elevated eyebrow of enquiry.

"Please," said Jo, feeling that speaking may overcome the queasy feeling of anticipation she was experiencing, "no sugar for either of us, just a little milk if we may?"

Audible from an out-of-view office was an authoritative voice, telling it like it is to an unfortunate caller. Dan picked up an elderly copy of The Cricketer from a dated teak coffee table, and Jo sipped her strong, bitter coffee. She was trying to compose herself and make her story sound believable while fending off an attack of self-doubt and confusion caused by tension.

Will paced from his office looking, to Dan, every inch the opening bowler on the cover of The Cricketer. He held out a strong, steady hand to Jo.

"Miss Hadge, I'm very pleased to welcome you, but I'm sure you are not so happy to be here," he smiled his best it-will-be-alright smile. "And you are Mr Rackham, good to meet you."

Dan returned the greeting with a firm handshake, and the two clients followed their lawyer to his office.

Real leather upright chairs, probably Hedge & Co originals from the 1920s, surrounded a mahogany dining table now serving as a client meeting desk. Will sagged down into his modern swivel chair by a more contemporary desk which did little to reflect the orderly mind of its user.

"Okay, Jo," said Will, looking directly into Jo's eyes. "You've got to understand straight away that this is going to be a long, worrying and uncomfortable process. I wish I could make it less so, but I can't. I also can't guarantee that you will walk away a free woman. We will do our very best for you, but there are no certainties. If you choose to appoint Hedge & Co to represent you, we will do so with all our skill and vigour and will expect that you work with us openly, honestly and cooperatively. Sometimes clients don't like doing what we ask or tell them to do, and that can make the whole process even more difficult than it already is." Will paused with an expectant expression directed at Jo.

"I understand," said Jo. "Dan selected Hedge & Co, and I realise I have to collaborate fully with you through this awful mess. I still don't understand how fighting off a drunken lout on my doorstep can result in my being the aggressor and him being the victim, and, let me tell you, I'll do whatever I have to do to prove my case." She finished with a tremor in her voice, a tear prickling the back of her eye.

"Quite so," responded Will, "That's the spirit, and don't take that as a condescension, you will have to find a lot of inner strength to prove your point in court, but, for now, that is a long way off, and we have a great deal to do between then and now.

"I have copies of all the statements so far from the police and a copy of the charge statement from the CPS. There is a very tiny chance we can get the CPS to drop this, so the first job for me, assuming you want Hedge & Co to represent you, is for me to try it on with them on the 'you can't win this' basis and see where we go. On the face of it, there is a self-defence position which looks very strong, but the fact that you stabbed the man with a kitchen knife and very nearly killed him suggests that you planned the attack because you had the knife in your hand when you opened the door to him, and we have only your word that you didn't recognise him through your front door peephole."

"If I say I didn't see him or anything else through the spyhole, then I bloody well didn't," said Jo, almost shouting in frustration and fearful anger, "and you'd better believe me, or I have no hope, no chance."

"As it stands," said Will, looking stern, "the police are still collecting evidence and statements, and the CPS is still building its prosecution case. We can't do much until we see all of the prosecution's case bundle; we just have to sit, wait and plan our defence. There are two factors we must consider now. The first is for us to go through your statement word by word and ensure that our defence argument is bullet-proof; for that to happen, we will need to arrange a session with our barrister, Simon Farrow. The second is to prepare, not that it takes much preparation, for your pre-trial plea hearing. For this, you will only need to turn up at Reading magistrates' courts near the Hexagon. All you'll have to do in court is confirm your name and your plea. It'll take minutes, and they often take the plea hearing first, so we should be top of the list and be in and out within an hour. If we aren't listed early, we could be there from 9.30 until half-past three or even four o'clock, Ok?"

Feeling more confident now the conversation was taking an active and positive tone, Jo replied, "Well, first off, I'd like to confirm that you and your barrister colleague will represent me, and I thank you for doing this. I must say I'm feeling a bit better about it all already, and yes, I understand what we have to do now. When will the magistrates' court hearing be?"

"We should have a date already, but the local police haven't supplied it to me yet. I'll call them today and confirm we are acting for you and get the date. I'll let you know as soon as I know."

"Would it help," said Dan joining in for the first time, "if we write down a detailed version of exactly what happened, based on Jo's statement, of course, but with any added info or detail we can remember? We could add our ideas of what the key defence arguments might be for you and the barrister to consider. It might save a lot of time when we next meet?"

"Yep," replied Will, looking at Dan with an appraising glance, "that might be useful."

Picking up a vague indifference, Dan added, "It would also help if we can have copies of all the evidence and statements you have now and whatever you get as it comes through from the police or CPS."

"Yes, of course," answered Will, who recognised Dan as sensible and intelligent, unlike the usual noisy, belligerents he so often had to suffer. Will didn't tolerate many people and people he regarded as witless, even less so.

"I'll be in touch as soon as I have the plea hearing date and whenever I get more through from the police and CPS. The good news, Jo, about all this is that we get to see everything the opposition has in its arsenal before we go into court, there are no surprises, no traps, and no clever tricks like you might see on the TV. We go in fully prepared and thoroughly planned and have the best chance we can possibly have. I'd like to say don't worry, but that's not likely; of course, you'll worry, but we'll do the best we can for you, and Simon knows what he's doing in court. As I say, there are no guarantees, but you are in safe hands, really you are.

"I understand, Jo, that you are self-employed and earn a decent amount, so I'm afraid there's no chance of getting legal aid for you. You'll have to pay for our services, of course, but in cases like this, where there is a realistic defence case that is comparatively easy to compile, we can be pretty keen on fees and will keep your bill down to the minimum. It will add up to several thousand, maybe as much as 10k depending on how much time we end up using and whether there are any added fees, costs or expenses we don't yet know about. I should also tell you now that if you are found innocent, you don't stand a chance in hell of getting any costs awarded. There is a rigmarole we could go through, but it won't work and will just cost you more in fees from us. I know this all sounds a bit bleak, but I have to be upfront about it. Ok?"

"Ok," said Jo.

"Ok, said Dan.

More handshakes, back to the lift and down to the street and the light, the noise and the somehow less pressurised atmosphere of the town outside.

Next to Hedge & Co's front door stood Il Caffe Bar, a very English version of an Italian coffee shop, which looked like a useful post-meeting refuge to Dan and Jo. Dan gripped Jo's sagging shoulders and guided her to a table for two in the window.

Coffee ordered and very necessary trips to the loo completed, Dan looked lovingly at Jo. He wished he could scoop up her sagging spirits as easily as he could grip her shoulders.

"Good man, I reckon," was Dan's opening comment of reassurance. "Seemed strong, professional and very sharp. Worth the money. I'll talk to Spray; we could get the company to pay it p'raps. Seems being innocent still carries a punishment, eh? Anyway, my Jo, what do you think?"

A frisson of pleasure ran through Jo at Dan's use of a possessive. She felt a much-needed sense of comfort and a new strength from knowing that she had all the support she could want.

"Actually, I liked him a lot. Straight, no fluff and nonsense and clearly not to be buggered about with and that's just what I need from a solicitor," said Jo, smiling a little for the first time that day.

"Yep, I agree," said Dan, "I have always found that solicitors don't do anything unless you tell them what to do but with Will, I think we have a proactive lawyer, and that's bloody good news 'cos they are pretty rare."

The two of them sat in the window and people-watched for a while, drifting through random thoughts of what might lie ahead.

Eventually, Dan said what Jo had been thinking, "Bewildering how one minute life is smooth and happy and then next you are in total turmoil and living through a nightmare. How does it happen so fast? How does it happen with absolutely no input from us, just happenstance? Quite astonishing and bloody frightening but actually, don't know about you but I feel much more optimistic now than I did when we arrived here. Wonder what this fellow Simon is like; if Will rates him, I suspect he's pretty shit hot, hope so anyway."

Jo nodded. "I still wake up in the morning and wonder why I feel so worried; it seems impossible that this is happening to me. Then I get furious that the feds and crappy CPS see fit to make me the baddy. Will and his chum had better be pretty bloody brilliant, that's what I say. Come on, Dan, let's go home. Can we go to your place tonight, please? I don't want to be on my own, and I don't want to see that damn front door again until tomorrow."

10

Slicko, as Sniff had named him, was Max Golby. In his mid-thirties, smart in mind and dress, Max was the walking definition of hedonism; an excellent example of amour-propre, Max created a self-image suggested by the lies he told himself about himself. He emulated Dan in his dress with handmade shirts, suits and shoes for work and wore trendy but safe styles from Tom Ford and J. Crew for casual. With a post-hipster beard, a carefully tended quiff hairstyle and half an arm of ink, Max willingly believed his own myth.

Morals and conscience were not uppermost in Max's list of preferred personal attributes. They had never been. The only son of a telecom engineer dad and a call centre mum, Max was loved and indulged throughout his childhood and teen years. Bright enough to be academically worthwhile, Max's natural indolence defeated any scholastic flair. Although he'd never know it, Max and Sniff had early years' experiences in common. They both learned to survive with minimal effort and to maximise any opportunity. Sniff chose the usual route of a convicted criminal which was to re-offend, while Max chose to follow a modified epithet, 'We neither weave nor spin, we merely manipulate.'

Max left school for a place at de Montford University, formerly Leicester Polytechnic, to study Electronic Engineering. After eighteen months of partying and some studying, Max was awarded a placement at Falco-Akron's European UK HQ in Belper. To begin with, Max's job was to prepare machines from the US for UK customers. It was easy but interesting work for Max, who found an unexpected enthusiasm for the 'mission-critical,' highly engineered computers.

Falco-Akron's customers were all in the aerospace, military, defence or law enforcement sectors. Although applications in these clients were diverse, a strong, influential user group was dedicated to working with the manufacturer further to develop the systems' technological leadership, especially against hacking, denial of service, and protocol integrity.

It was at the 'FalAk' conference at the Grand Hotel Krasnapolsky in Amsterdam where, as the on-call technical support engineer, Max met Spray Wilson. The conference bar, set under the arches of the hotel's 19th-century style Winter Garden, was quiet as those on European time had drifted away after a hectic day, to change for the conference gala dinner. Spray, who had been travelling for weeks, quite literally didn't know the time of day and Max was happy to hobnob with anyone who might be useful.

It was Max's 'FalAk, Just Do It' T-shirt that kicked off the conversation. "Good attitude, man," muttered Spray, partly to his bourbon and

partly to the wearer.

"I'd say so," said Max earnestly, turning up his English accent for the sake of the apparent American. "I jolly well live by it I can tell you. That's why I'm here; if anything goes wrong and needs fixing, well, I just do it!"

"That right?" drawled Spray, picking up on the native accent emphasis and replying in kind. "How about we get this great gal here to fix us another drink?"

"Oh, cheers chum," Max would have wagged his tail if he'd had one.

"S'Ok man," said Spray, quietly amusing himself now, "I s'ppose we've gotta get properly sociable for tonight's shindig, let's sip some sauce and p'raps it'll look more 'pealin'."

Several drinks later, Spray and Max agreed that a conference gala dinner, talking in binary code with clever geeks, had lost all possible appeal. The delights of Dam Square and surrounding windowed streets beckoned instead.

It was as they walked past the 'Hash Marihuana and Hemp

Museum' that Spray expressed an interest in psychoactive drugs, and Max, who smoked a little cannabis but lacked any greater experience, agreed with a vigorous nod, wondering where such a conversation may lead. It led to a bright shop and café where hash and paddos, from the Dutch paddestoel for mushroom, were on offer, together with coffee and Jonge Jenever gin.

Very drunk and stoned too, Max told Spray that he was ambitious, amenable and unquestioning for the right rewards. Spray told Max that Onetelcall held more potential for profit than 'those Akron assholes' and that he'd have a word with his COO Dan in Olderbury, if Max might be interested? Max affirmed his interest, and Spray looked knowingly, through blurring eyes, at the young, malleable Englishman.

Max next saw Spray the following day. Spay was very much the dynamic CEO. He postured around the speaker's stage, sharing the finer technological points of the Onetelcall integrated security superiority with his attentive audience. Feeling sick, hung-over and a little shaky, Max was impressed by the man's resilience and energy and, even more, had a feeling that sometime in the haze of the previous night, he had been offered something a little more than a job.

Spray went straight to the neighbouring 'The Tailor' bar after his presentation. In this more discrete sanctuary away from delegates, he ordered a beer and a large bourbon to replace his diminishing speaker performance adrenaline. Settled in a plush, blue suede sofa, Spray mentally replayed last night's conversation with Max. Even through the murk of intoxication, Spray recognised the chancer, the amoral buccaneer that Max so obviously was. Untrustworthy? Certainly. Bright and able to tap-dance through darker machinations? Yep, seems so. Smart enough to live two roles? Probably. Worth the risk but must carry built-in contingency. Comebacks can't happen. Hey, give it a whirl.

"Dan, buddy, how you doing?" Spray enquired by phone from his sumptuous hiding place as another huge bourbon was delivered. "Gotta young dude I'd like you to see, met him at this

FalAk gig, and I reckon he'd be a good incoming goods manager for you. If I give him your number, will you check him out?"

Within a month, Max had a job offer from Onetelcall, and he started straight away. You don't stay a moment longer at Falco Akron once you've given in your resignation.

Max moved from Derbyshire to Olderbury and took a lease on a small but stylish flat in a converted farm building two miles away from the town. Having a place of his own was a new experience for Max, who had been what he liked to describe as a hobosexual pillow surfer. This meant finding girls with their own homes and moving in until the magic wore off or a better bet came along, usually via the more casual dating sites.

He settled into Onetelcall quickly and soon became popular in the company and the town. During the day, he worked as hard as required. He fitted in well with the rest of the inbound, preparation and distribution teams and reined in his previous naturally arrogant and sarcastic tendencies.

At night he took the more sophisticated or impressionable girls he met to Olderbury's better restaurants; the more amenable, less demanding dates got the Chinese takeaway and instant seduction treatment in Max's customised-for-purpose bachelor lair. He had installed an AI voice control system for all the flat's functions, lighting, sounds, heating, scent-emitters, screen, video and music, and used his trick toys to full effect on his vulnerable prey.

Max was not a habitual pub-goer but did call into the town's more civilised places occasionally if only to widen his hunting ground and meet more people who might one day be useful. However, although slightly rough for his tastes, Max did go to Olderbury's two nightclubs, usually on Friday nights.

Z-Space was the most happening, at least that's how it described itself. Set in the disused warehouses behind the Market Square arcade, Z-Space extended over three floors and featured fire-eaters and pyrotechnics as well as VIP and quieter eating areas. It kaboomed house, chart and R&B music relentlessly.

Hana Hou Bar was a Hawaiian-themed nightspot with everything designed for the social media moment. A very connected enterprise, 'H-H' didn't need to spend on publicity, its customers did the job splendidly with every party posting every memorable moment on Tik-Tok, Instagram, WhatsApp, Facebook, Twitter et al. 'H-H' was popular for hen-nights, stag nights, multi-nights and birthday parties. It also staged singles-only parties 'with added aloha' where 'Hawaiian Lei' took on a homophonic meaning.

Saying goodbye to Daphne – it was Daphne, wasn't it? Or was it Danni? - on a Saturday morning, Max had a rare moment of reflection; a good place to live, lots of female company, a good job and a decent income, life was sweet.

He stooped to pick up an envelope from his anti-trend welcome mat. The exclusively digital Max regarded anything hand-written and traditionally posted in a letterbox as a complete anachronism. He found reading from anything but a screen oddly uncomfortable, something to be saved for his dotage perhaps. Max didn't know anyone who would write a letter and was intrigued, even more so when he noticed the USA airmail stamp.

He opened the envelope and extracted a single sheet of old-fashioned typewritten paper. It read:

This is the most secure message you can get. Untraceable.

A consignment is coming to you from Medina on Tuesday – usual shippers, usual delivery, nothing to notice or create any interest.

Box OTC11-B/C. Open it, take out the poly-bubble pack and keep it. Treat everything else in the box as usual. Just keep the poly bubble safe and separate. Someone will contact you on Wednesday. He will say OTC poly-bubble. You give it to him. You get five hundred pounds in cash from him.

If you feel like sharing this note with anyone – and I mean anyone at all - check your email first. Want to be a culprit? If you refuse to do this, it's Ok but you may need another job. If it goes well, then we'll go places together.

Before he could consider all the implications of this astonishing note, Max reached for his phone to see his emails. He could smell an implied threat and felt a sudden stomach-drop fear. "Check your email first" ... "be a culprit." It didn't sound good. Max thought he recognised a fit-up in the making.

In the usual array of expected emails and everyday quick correspondence, Max saw an unusual word: **EMBARGOED.**

He opened the text and read what appeared to be a press release:

The office of The CEO, Onetelcall, Medina.

Onetelcall is to launch a major investigation into allegations of drug trafficking and money laundering in its UK and European facilities.

Working openly with national and international drug enforcement agencies, Onetelcall will determine quickly and transparently whether transgressions of any laws have been organised by any of the company's personnel.

Any colleagues found to be associated with any illegal activity will be handed to the relevant authorities without delay.

Onetelcall CEO Spray (Ray) Wilson said: "We are a security company with clients around the world who entrust the safety and impenetrability of their business processes to our technology. I will not have any allegations of illegal activity associated with the company we have built and of which we are all so proud. Any rogue employee or employees will be dealt with mercilessly by us and, I'm sure, by the appropriate authorities."

For further details....

Max stood on his homely mat, holding a letter in one hand

and his phone in the other and wondered what the hell was happening to him. He needed to think clearly; threat or opportunity, or both?

He felt alone. Max was used to being in tight spots, more usually with irate husbands and dodgy gambling creditors, this was different. He wasn't sure how to handle a powerful, probably sociopathic Machiavellian drug baron who could undoubtedly arrange sufficient evidence to be created to ensure Max would be locked up.

Who could he turn to? Obviously, Dan, whom Max had come to like and respect, was ignorant of the illicit import business he was unknowingly fronting. Whatever Spray was up to, he'd probably been at it for some time without any hint of rumour or suspicion. The fact that he was being asked to do so little suggested he would be a new cog in an established, and therefore probably invulnerable, organisation. And five hundred pounds in cash? 'Go places together?' What choice did he have? He asked himself, as dreams of easy riches lit up his gambler's synapses. For Max, the old online warning to 'gamble responsibly' put the moron into oxymoron.

Increasing excitement gradually vanquished doubts, and when Tuesday arrived, Max was light-headed and tense with excitement. Anticipation, however, was more exciting than the eventual occurrence. As his job included being incoming goods manager, Max, saw his team preparing for the day's delivery of components transported by sea from Medina to Port of London and then by secure courier from the City to Olderbury.

The goods reception area was as clinically immaculate as a hospital operating theatre, white and stainless steel with daylight floodlighting the whole area. A truck backed up to a drape-protected roller door and lowered its tailgate to the elevated delivery platform. A delivery-zone-only forklift slowly slid its prongs under each of the seven pallets and, one by one carried the lorry's load past sophisticated scanners into Onetelcall's UK goods reception unit.

"Don't see you down here very often, boss," said forklift driver Ian to his urbane-looking manager.

"New security check," said Max. "I want to do some random checks on some of these boxes," he added, trying to sound relaxed and in charge.

"Oh, that again," smiled Ian. "We used to run spot checks for ages, I never really knew why. It was a pet project of the manager before you came along. What do you want me to do?"

Max's interest was piqued. "What was the object of the old checks then, Ian? What was the other chap looking for?"

"No idea, Max. He was very fussy and secretive, like one of us was some sort of thief. Some of us didn't like it too much, but nothing ever came up from any of his searches and, to be honest, we all ended up thinking he was just a bit of a jobsworth pratt."

Max smiled at his colleague. "I see, well, I'll tell you exactly why I'm doing random checks, it's because some of the bozos in Medina have been slapping the wrong code numbers on the wrong boxes, which causes more confusion than I need and as I get the bollockings when items get misplaced, I'm going to make sure blame get redirected to where it should be, in bloody Ohio."

Ian, who enjoyed other people being criticised because it meant he wasn't in the firing line for a change, grinned in tacit agreement. "Oki-koki Max, which boxes do you want to look at?"

Max gave him a series of identity codes, casually including OTC11-B/C and asked, "What happened to the manager before me then, Ian?"

"Good question," replied the forklift driver. "He was an odd bugger, always seemed a bit spaced out. We all thought he might have had a bit of a habit if you know what I mean. Anyway, he didn't fit in all that well, couldn't have a laugh with him, know what I mean, like we do with you. Anyway, one day he was here, next day he was gone, not a word of see-ya or anything, just gone. Dan popped down to tell us he'd gone; like we hadn't noticed already, but didn't tell us anything more. I think he was as surprised as we were, and we could tell he'd no idea where he'd gone either, so we just cracked on as normal with Dan. He's a good bloke he is, coming in when deliveries were due just to make sure we was all Ok and then, well, that's how it was until you appeared."

Max's gut tightened with a cold suspicion of what might have happened to his predecessor, and the realisation that he was walking along a dangerous one-way road gripped him.

After giving a few decoy boxes his fullest attention, Max opened his target consignment and, ensuring he wasn't being watched, quickly and surreptitiously removed the large poly-bubble wrapping sleeve.

"This looks wrong, I think," said Max, pointing at the security sticker on the poly-bubble. "I'll take it and check. Fingers crossed we've got a winner," he added conspiratorially to his colleague.

Ian grinned again in knowledgeable approval as his manager strolled off, lugging the surprisingly weighty and voluminous packaging.

Max's office was a half-height, blue-panelled partitioned area of about three by three metres containing his stand-or-sit workstation, two grey fabric visitor chairs and bright-white filing and storage unit. He ensured the poly-wrap was out of sight to any passer-by and looked at it, wondering what, when, how and why.

Apart from wondering what would happen next in the immediate future, Max was worried about what would happen next in the longer term. More consignments, more poly-bubble, more cash? Or a sudden and mysterious exit? He had little choice other than to follow his luck and play the game to the best of his ability. He looked at the small mirror pinned to a partition panel and tried to reassure himself with a cocky wink and trigger-finger gesture. I'm on my way to big money, he thought, driving his doubts away.

He inspected the poly-bubble packaging again. It was a heavy, high-performance barrier, solid black polymer lamination which protected whatever it surrounded from static and penetrating x-rays or scanners. Like an inflatable Lilo, corrugated tube shapes seamed together to make a folded cube of six panels, each about a metre square to fit the cardboard outer from which Max had taken them. How many bags of flour could I squeeze into those tubes? wondered Max, knowing without being told that he had in his hands a small fortune in cocaine. At a sale price of something like £50 per gram, Max reckoned each of the six panels probably contained at least one kilo of loose powdered 'bricks' which would be, say, six kilos, and that would be… Christ, that would be, fuckin' hell, a street price of… oh dear God, that's £300,000!

His work mobile sounded with an urgent buzz. "It's Max," he answered, "how can I help you?"

"OTC poly-bubble," said a gruff, semi-disguised man's voice.

"Yep," said Max, "what about it? thought I'd get this call tomorrow. What's going on?"

"Yeah," drawled the bucolic voice, "don't want you to have time to get nosey, wouldn't be good for you. That pack better be in one piece wiv no holes, understand?"

"It's here and all as it should be," replied Max, "and don't threaten me, understand?"

Let's get going on the front foot, thought Max, feeling not quite as brave as he hoped he'd sounded.

"Back door to your car park, the black fire door closest to the bins, at exactly four on the nose, no fuckin' me about and be on time."

"No," asserted Max, thinking he'd push back to see what response he'd get, "it's getting busy out there by four. I'll be at the back door at three-fifteen if you want your er- goods, you'll be there too. Clear enough for you?"

The voice hesitated, and Max could feel his caller wasn't used to negotiating. "Makes sense I s'ppose," said the voice, "quarter past three it is."

After the call, Max took the Loden coat he kept in his office, just in case of bad weather or a need to adopt a suave persona and wrapped it around his valuable packaging. If he carried it casually, over his arm, it looked normal.

Max's walking-on-thin-ice instincts told him to take a hiding-in-plain-sight approach. He walked upright and boldly past Onetelcall HQ's internal cameras and marched to the back door like a man with a job to do. He looked at his Baume et Mercier watch and, at fourteen minutes past three, opened the black back door and looked out to the car park. In the reserved spaces were Dan's yellow BMW, his own slightly older S3 Audi and a collection of employees' cars. An old, once silver, now grey Ford moved slowly and noisily towards Max.

Leaning across to open the passenger door window by its manual winder, a tired and inconsequential-looking middle-aged man looked at Max. "OTC-,"

"Here," interrupted Max, wanting this exchange to be as brief as possible. He thrust his coat through the window and deposited the thick black poly packaging onto the Escort's passenger seat. "You've got something for me then?" he said, withdrawing his coat.

Duggie reached inside his jacket in an almost comically exaggerated way and extracted a thick manilla envelope. Of course, thought Max, it had to be a brown envelope. This was getting like a bad movie. He accepted the envelope and adroitly tucked it under his coat as he turned away.

11

Reading Magistrates Court had the look and smell of all public buildings. Officious people paraded their lanyards and clutched important bits of paper as they hithered and thithered. Curt, uniformed security guards displayed their authority with gratuitous disdain as they scanned and frisked today's batch of customers.

Huddles of pale, weakened, demoralised-looking visitors searched the pinboards for their names and courtroom numbers. Solicitors strutted their condescension as they shepherded their flocks of flotsam into quiet discussion areas, told them what would happen next and how to behave themselves if they knew what was good for them.

Those without professional representation gathered in gangs; some laughed loudly, masking their apprehension and fear, others pale and tense gazed unseeingly, worrying, imagining the worst. Some more experienced offenders sauntered up and down with an affected swagger, knowing they were about to get another fine they wouldn't pay.

In an overwhelmingly depressing dark green and brown collection area, stained vinyl chairs became strangely appealing sanctuaries for Dan and Jo's nervous, unsteady legs.

"Good morning you two," smiled a dapper-looking Will, "welcome to the factory. I've had a word with the clerk; we're in court two. We'll be up third in the list, there are just two cases before us, both remands, so we might be out by ten or so."

"Hello, Will, how are you?" smiled Jo, hiding her apprehension. "To be out of here by ten would be wonderful. It's really dismal, isn't it?"

"It isn't supposed to be a fun-filled place, Jo, although I must say it amuses me from time to time; but no, it isn't that appealing.

Anyway, I assume that you aren't doing anything else this morning as you might have expected to be here all day, so I think we should go back to the office when we are finished here and review our position. We've got most of the prosecution bundle now."

It took only seven minutes for the magistrate to ask Jo to confirm her identity and to read the formal charge of inflicting grievous bodily harm with intent to cause grievous bodily harm as described by section 18 of the Offences against the Person Act (1861). The magistrate explained that the offence attracts a penalty of between 3 and 16 years imprisonment and asked her to plead guilty or not guilty.

Reeling at the length of the possible prison terms, Jo managed to say "not guilty" without stammer or stutter. PC Amanda Cotter was the only witness, there to confirm that the police would allow bail on the usual conditions, including reporting to Olderbury police station once every week until the court hearing.

Leaving the dour brick building and walking out onto the terrace which led to Reading's Hexagon Theatre, Jo felt as though she was fleeing a condemned cell. Breathing deeply, she grasped Dan's ready, resolute arm and felt a sense of relief flow through her.

"Wasn't so bad, eh?" asked Dan gently.

"Could have been much worse, that's for sure," she replied, noticing that Will and PC Amanda Cotter were walking together towards Broad Street Mall. "Those two look thick as thieves. I thought she seemed quite nice on the quiet, wonder what they're talking about."

"You'll soon be able to ask him," said Dan. "We'll see if we can sneak in a quick take-away coffee when we get there; anything's better than Hedges' muck."

Coffees in hand, Dan and Jo met Will by the lift to his offices.

"Sorry," said Dan, "do you want one?" indicating his disposable coffee carton.

Will stood aside to let Jo into the lift.

"You and the young policewoman seem friendly," said Jo with a slight smirk.

"Actually," responded Will stiffly, "she a decent young copper who knows more than she lets on and keeps her cards close to her chest most of the time, although she has been useful in tipping us a nod when we've needed it in the past. I'm sure she's Ok, but you can never be too sure with the local police. Shouldn't say that should I, but in this case, I do think that Amanda has a strong view about what's happening to you, and I don't think she altogether approves."

Back at his desk, Will produced the CPS bundle, a thick file of witness statements, medical reports and other relevant - and some irrelevant - documents.

"Simon and I have had a cursory run through all this; we didn't get it all until yesterday, which is very late considering. Anyway, we've looked at it and, to be honest, it's a bit thin. We are surprised the CPS is going for it, but going for it they undoubtedly are, I'm sorry to say."

Jo was looking downcast and left it to Dan to say,

"What possible evidence can they have that Jo is guilty of anything or that this bloody Sniff oik isn't guilty as sin of molesting her?"

"OK, I know how you feel but this is serious stuff, and they appear to be building a case around the very serious bit which is 'intent.' Of course, the prosecution has to prove guilt and get a jury to agree. We don't, as such, have to prove innocence but even so, we need to build a robust defence, and I have to say right now, nothing is a foregone conclusion, we've got a lot of work to do."

"Can we go through what you've got so far?" asked Dan.

"Oh yes, I've had everything copied so you can take a complete file away with you. But there is some evidence which doesn't look too good for us, for instance, there is some evidence that you've known Sniff – er, Kevin Taylor to be correct – for some time and have a personal relationship with him, Jo?"

"What? What absolute rot, what are you saying?" Jo raised her voice in annoyance.

"Yes, Jo," continued Will, "that's what the evidence suggests. They've been busy have the police. Don't know where they find the resources for such investigation when there's so much real work for them to do, but they have come up with lots of statements I wasn't expecting." He shuffled through a wad of stapled sets of papers. "Such as two members of staff from The Royal George hotel who have said that they saw you and Taylor together at a gala dinner a few months ago; the landlord of The Carpenters Arms who says you and Taylor had drinks together there; the manager of the Biggabookie betting shop who says you and Taylor were in there laughing away about a winner you'd both backed; Taylor's friend Duggie Miller who claims you and Taylor have a bit of a thing going...."

"Enough, enough!" yelled Jo. "This is preposterous, total lies, bunkum, rubbish, lies, lies... where, I mean, how on earth can this be... good God, a thing... what sort of thing, disgusting little man, a thing... Christ almighty."

"We haven't seen anything yet, but we also believe the CPS will have some form of photo or video evidence to support all this, so we need to be very careful about what we say, what we admit, what we refute and how we position you and Taylor in terms of whether you knew or know one-another and just what sort of relationship you had or have. I have to be sure we cover all the bases, Jo," explained Will.

"We understand that Will," said Dan in his calm, objective way, "but it is clear some form of snow job is turning into a blizzard here. I can tell you now that there is no relationship between Jo and this man, but I understand that we have to be able to repudiate it totally and demonstrably."

"Quite so," agreed Will, "and I'm afraid there's more. It seems the CPS have a tame expert witness who's ready to say in court that the nature of the wound inflicted on Taylor suggests premeditation and an intent to cause maximum injury without actually causing death, and that's a dangerous claim for us to fight off. Mention death and any jury go straight into hyperdrive, it seems there's something big and romantic about being on a snuff jury."

"Bloody marvellous, so now Jo is some female philandering would-be murderess, and the CPS is going to make a jury feel like TV stars in some courtroom saga, is that it?" Dan was feeling outraged for Jo and wanted to show it.

"Yep," said Will, his sharp eyes narrowing, "but it's no snow job that will melt away; at least that's how it seems at the moment and, you know this, I have to ask right now two questions which you won't like one little bit, but I'm asking anyway."

He looked at Jo steadily and unemotionally as he put his questions.

"Jo, did you know Taylor before the incident, and did you take careful aim before you stabbed your knife in?"

Calm and business-like again now, Jo looked straight into her lawyer's enquiring eyes and answered, "I did come across the horrid man at a sort of works event. I was a guest of the organisers at The Royal George. I have seen him around town, I know who he is because the MD of the company at the gala event said his name was Sniff and that he was a dodgy bit of work to be avoided at all costs. He was pretty cross that Sniff was there at all. And I did see him again in Biggabookie when I popped in there to get some cash from their ATM. It's a cash machine in the shop, not on the outside wall as usual, so I was in there when he was. We certainly weren't sharing a laugh or anything else, come to that. Not sure when I was last in The Carps, I think it's a grubby, scrotty dump with a misery of a landlord; I don't like it all. Still, I have been in there, it's true, that's all that's true though, and as for a relationship, candidly, will you look at him and then look at Dan? Tell me you think it's likely?" Jo paused for breath, almost hyperventilating, taut with the effort of explaining herself.

"Look Will," said Dan, "would I be right in suggesting that Jo and I leave now and go through all this? We can prepare all of the answers and make some points of our own to offer, and then, perhaps, it would be best to meet again when we can get together with your barrister too?"

"Spot on, Dan," replied Will, "that's exactly what needs to happen next. And just to be clear, there are no other options here; we are not going to get the CPS to climb down now; someone's neck will be on the line and saving face is what matters in that department. Also, I'm not planning on spending any of your money on any private investigators to prove or disprove any of Taylor's claims or any other evidence. We need to be as... er... fiscally prudent as possible because, I can tell you now, we are in for a three-day hearing at least, even if the CPS drops half of its witnesses."

Dan picked up the CPS copy file with one hand and Jo's slightly shaking hand with the other. They said their goodbyes to Will and headed, via the small, creaking lift, down to street level and the sanctuary of Il Caffe for their now habitual loo visit and some more coffee.

Dan opened the file, and on top of the traditionally ribbon-tied bundle was the CPS 'Regina v Joanna Hadge' Statement/Evidence list. Dan scanned the list, wondering how a computer-generated document could look like it was produced on a historic manual typewriter.

Kevin Taylor
Douglas Miller
Kirk Robinson
Arthur Perry
Eric Woods
Peggy Woods
Tom Alderton
James Ansell
Susan Clark
John Mayhew
David Gordon
Sgt P283 Mick Cowan
PC P7976Thomas
PC P7654 Pitt
WPC P7766 Cotter
Kim Joiner (SOCO)
Dr Philip Drake (Expert witness)

A&E report

CCTV*

*Not available.

As Jo returned from the ladies, she was surprised to see Dan looking amused. A slant of her head asked why.

"This is like the cast of an Agatha Christie murder," he grinned, "Jo Hadge, in the hall with a chopper."

"Not funny, you arse," responded Jo. "You'll be minus your chopper if you decide this is all a source for more of your jokes. I'm really worried. Just look at that file; someone's been putting in a lot of work to make a big case against me by the look of it."

"Seems that way, Jo, I must admit. Lots of statements, and lots of evidence. So, I suppose the job now is to go through it all and give this Simon QC chap our best attempt at providing him with defence bullets to shoot. Let's give it a go, eh? Doing something positive can only make you feel better."

They spent two hours and four coffees running through the sheaves of verbiage, most of which seemed like it came from a parallel universe.

"This man Taylor is a snivelling liar, isn't he, no wonder he's called Sniff," murmured a saddened Jo. "How do we fight against complete fabrication like this?"

"This is the moment when I should say something like 'just tell the truth,' but right now I just don't know what to say, it's unbelievable to the extent that it just may be believable to a jury, you know, the bigger the lie and all that," Dan looked downcast. "Will's barrister man had better be all he says he is, that's all I can say."

Dan reached across the table and grasped Jo's hand. He felt sorrow, he felt protective, something deeper than lust and affection.

"You know Jo, this oik Sniff Taylor is just that, an oik and any jury will surely see that. We can't be intimidated by his lies, for God's sake, we're supposed to be smart, cleverer than the average type Y-genners, so let's get back on our game and work out how to show just what a disgusting example of neo-humanity Taylor is."

Jo squeezed Dan's fingers and smiled a wan but bright smile which didn't quite succeed.

"OK, let's look at the dramatis personae. We know Kevin Tylor is Sniff, and I can see that Kirk Robinson is that Lardy character and Arthur Perry is Arfa, obviously, although I thought it might have meant arfa a mind, arf-arf."

"Remember your chopper, Dan...."

"Sorry, onwards. Eric and Peggy from The Carps we know, I know Tom Alderton, he's a good chap, ambulance you know, and clearly David Gordon is from The Coopers across the road from you."

"Yeah," Jo joined in. "James Ansell is the manager of The Royal George, very suave but Ok nonetheless, and I worked with Sue, Susan Clark, at Raglan; at least these two will be truthful. The Mayhew person is from Biggabookie which leaves Douglas Miller. Do you know him? Cos I've absolutely no idea who he could be."

Dan shook his head, "No, I don't know him, but he makes some pretty wild claims about your relationship with Taylor. He must be a stooge of some sort. I have no idea, either, why CCTV is listed but isn't available. Is it from the bookie? From the pub? I mean, where is it from, and what does it show? I'm a bit worried that the CPS lists it but might be withholding it as some form of crafty strategy. Could it show something slightly incriminating, I wonder?"

"Like what for heaven's sake? There's nothing incriminating it could show, is there?"

"No, Jo, of course not, there can't be. Let's jack it in now and go home. Yours or mine?"

12

Simon Farrow looked like an overgrown choir boy. Approaching forty, he could still be a ten-year-old with straw-coloured, tightly curled hair, blue eyes and pale skin with red-blotch cheeks; his beard was fair and not the stuff of designer stubble. Despite his angelic looks, Simon was as tough as they come mentally, a little less so physically. Looking like a cherub had made for a hard early life, and he had learned quickly how to deal with the pains of verbal and physical assault. Simon went to an exclusive private school until a sudden dip in his parents' fortune dictated a transfer from the cushioned elite to a hard, violent comprehensive. Simon had been picked on for being the poor boy at a posh school and beaten up for being a posh kid at the poor school; his angelic looks had invited bullying attention from both ends of society's spectrum.

Despite being the antithesis of a young girl's fantasy date, Simon elicited a protective affection from the girls in the large mixed school who, unbidden, formed a defensive axis to keep his aggressors at bay. Make 'em laugh became Simon's strategy for survival, and his quick wit, sometimes gentle and kind, occasionally sardonic and incisively cutting, was an effective weapon against those less gifted tormentors. The beatings stopped, and a tougher, smarter young man emerged.

A little Latin from his previous school proved beneficial in Simon's development as an enthusiastic exponent of elegant English, and the secondary school's excellent English teacher nurtured his young protegee to be a proficient writer and speaker. University sped by in a whirl of exploring his libido and studying law. After qualifying, Simon took a pupillage in Manchester where he developed his barrister's courtroom and cross-examination skills, which were noted by the Court of Appeal. Simon moved on to a chambers' tenancy in Reading, specialising in fraud, GBH, robbery and serious drug offences.

He had been instructed by Will on several defence briefs, and it seemed a natural progression for the two men, who had become as close to friendship as either would allow, to work together for their joint greater good. In his efforts to elevate Hedges & Co to the rarer and enviable position of full-service criminal law, Will had made a junior partner of the younger barrister, Simon Farrow QC.

Simon loved being in court. He loved the theatre, the point and counterpoint, the psychology, the tactics and strategies, the excitement of winning and even the justice of the occasional loss when deserved. Most of all, Simon had a firm belief in the British justice system, if not always its sentencing policies. He always started his first meeting with new clients with his assurance that British justice will have its way. When Dan and Jo met him in the Hedges & Co offices, his opening gambit was one of reassurance.

"Jo, Dan, how good to meet you at last. I've been on your case since you first instructed Will, so I am fully cognisant of its complexities and evident contradictions. I know you must be feeling both aggrieved and threatened Jo, but I can assure you that our British justice system is fair, honest, effective and trustworthy; absolutely the best in the world."

"That's most comforting," replied a smiling Jo who had taken to her innocent-looking council at once. "If that's true, then I have nothing to worry about."

"True though it is, I must say, before any other comments are made, that there are no guarantees, ever, and I can give no guarantee now. I must make that very clear. Do I think you have a good case? Yes, of course, I do, and I know, yes know, you are innocent in a non-abstract way. In the specific charges and circumstances of those charges, we must be assiduous in our honesty and punctilious in our case preparation. I detect weaknesses in the CPS position, and such weaknesses make the prosecuting council even more motivated to go for the kill."

Seeing the clouds forming in Jo's eyes, Dan took the initiative,

"That's fully understood, Simon, we are not asking for guarantees, and we know that you'll provide the very best defence we can ask for, so let's move on and get down, as they say, to cases. We have gone through the CPS statement and evidence and written our answers, our thoughts and repudiations here."

He handed his defence documents to Simon. What had taken hours to prepare was speed-read by Simon in just a few minutes.

"OK, that's very helpful, yep, great, well done, thank you, yes, indeed." Simon was talking but it was obvious his mind was somewhere else.

"Simon? Is there anybody there?" whispered Jo.

"Oh, sorry, yes, hmmm, excuse me, just thinking about the accusations and your answers. It's like looking at two worlds through one keyhole. Victim, perpetrator, who is which? Old acquaintances, new enemies? Why did it happen at all? We need to see the CCTV before committing to a plan. But, Jo, I need to go through what will sound like the same old questions all over again. You know them all too well, they are these:

Why not call the police?

Why not call an ambulance?

Why open the door in the first place?

Why open it with a kitchen knife in your hand?

How well did you know Taylor?

Did you aim deliberately or just lunge?

Had you been taking cocaine?

Could you see Taylor through your front door spy hole?

And Dan, before you ask, I am casting aside any reference to the attack on you. It will confuse the jury, and although its inclusion may devalue any statements from Robinson and Perry, it will deflect the focus of our attack on Taylor."

"Ah," said Dan, delving into his backpack and pulling out a flask, "I expected this and, knowing your office coffee as I do, we bought this; it might be a little tastier. Would you like some?"

Fortified and emboldened by high-grade caffeine, the three new allies began the long, detailed and arduous task of step-by-stepping through the whole sorry tale until most, not all, answers were in place to Simon's satisfaction.

Jo, her mind at maximum acuity, wanted to add a new potential dimension to her position. She knew, as did most longer-term residents of Olderbury, that Taylor had been in court before, separately from the grassing and police-associated hearings. It had been for an accusation made by Taylor's former girlfriend that he had physically attacked her and her toddler child whilst temporarily living at her flat. The woman had asked for an injunction or a non-molestation order to protect her and her child from further abuse. Although the hearing had been held in chambers, the finding against Taylor was talk-on-the-streets of Olderbury within hours of being made.

"Everyone knows," explained Jo, "it is in the common, public domain, so surely, we can show that violence against women is in Taylor's history?"

"You'd think so, wouldn't you?" answered Simon. "But I'm afraid it's a no-go. There is such a thing as The Attorney General's Guidelines on Disclosure. If we decide to pop this bit of hearsay evidence into our defence, we'd be facing a retrial at best or even charges of contempt. Sorry and all that, but I'm afraid mum's the word on Taylor's previous until the jury has reached a decision."

Jo looked unconvinced, a rebellious expression that Dan knew well flicked across her face.

"Hmmm, I see, that's just stupid and unfair. If the man is a woman beater,

everyone should know he is. This is the law protecting a cowardly lout; it's just wrong, very wrong."

"It may seem that way at a superficial glance, Jo, but that's the way the law is at present, and it has worked for justice just as much as, sometimes, it would have appeared to impede it. Whatever our views, it is the way it is; we must abide by it or risk losing our defence and possibly a lot more."

"OK," conceded Jo reluctantly and unconvincingly. "Then there's little more we can say now, is there? Until we have sight of this much-vaunted CCTV, I suppose we must wait and hope."

Dan and Jo left Simon and headed for their loo and coffee sanctuary again.

"Blimey, that was a heavyweight session," sighed Jo, strained after all her painful recollections. "Simon is good, isn't he, you know, I do have faith in him, but I can't help but worry, it isn't as straightforward as it should be, is it?"

"He does seem like the real thing but, honestly, I think we have to be prepared for a highly skewed version of events from the prosecution. They've nailed their colours to the Taylor victim mast, and I expect they'll go all-out not to look as though they've fucked up. Simon may have faith in our judicial system, but I have no faith whatsoever in the CPS." He paused when he saw the blond-bubble-headed QC stride into Il Caffe.

"Ah, what-ho, esteemed clients," Simon smiled in professional friendliness. "Thought I'd find you two here, pop in myself for a decent coffee on the rare occasion of a spare moment. Anyway, do you have time to pop back up to the office? The CPS has just delivered a DVD of the CCTV."

They settled into a different office equipped with a DVD player and an older TV-style monitor. The disc played, and they saw a distant and indistinct image of Jo's street-level front door and the road in front of it. The field of vision was limited; it revealed only about 10ft on either side of the door and not as far as the corner of the road or the front of the pub.

"I see," said Dan, "this is the view from the pub's car park. Can you see, Simon? The camera is aimed at the car park entrance, but you can see right across to Jo's front door; that's handy then."

"It's more than handy, Dan," replied Simon, "it's a jury winner by the look of it so far. Let's let it run and see what happens."

The video image, a little indistinct and almost ethereal showed Sniff walking slowly and hesitantly from the direction of the corner and down the road towards Jo's front door.

"He looks pissed or stoned, or both," remarked Jo.

Sniff walked past the door and a little further down the street, out of shot. Seconds later, he reappeared. He walked across the road and back again. As he crossed back, he speeded up visibly and squared his shoulders from their customary slouch. That he was hammering insistently was obvious even without sound. His arm flailed against the door; his right foot made kicking motions. Light from the hallway began to show as Jo slowly opened the door. For a moment, the door was just ajar, and then it was suddenly fully open. Sniff appeared to be trying to walk in.

Jo was still invisible to the camera, but Sniff's wiry frame was clearly filling the doorway. An arm swung into shot; it was Jo's right arm, grainy and a little blurred, but there could be no doubt. The arm flashed forwards in an arc towards Sniff's advancing body. The arm concluded its swoop and Sniff appeared to halt, his left arm jumped up to his neck and his right arm thrust out towards Jo. Her left arm appeared in the lunging, driving action of a boxer's jab and Sniff seemed to lurch backwards. As he did so, the light from the hall began to diminish; Jo was pushing the door closed. Sniff took another aim at the door with his right foot and left arm but fell away quickly, still holding his neck.

In the final closing sequence, the door closed, the light extinguished, and Sniff limped away up the road towards the corner, towards the pub.

Dan looked impassive. Jo looked triumphant. Simon frowned.

"I can see that you think this proves your point, Jo," said Simon, "but if I were a prosecutor in this case, I'd claim that you took deliberate aim and intended to cause lethal harm to the victim. I'd work on the jury until the words 'victim', 'lethal', 'stabbing' and 'deliberate aim' were embedded in their minds." Simon paused as Jo looked increasingly horrified, "I know, I know, Jo, but we have to face facts and countenance the very worst; to underestimate now would be a serious error indeed."

"But you are my defence, Simon, surely you can see what happened, isn't it blindingly bloody obvious that I was being attacked by an out-of-his-mind yobbo?"

"Quite so Jo, quite so."

13

The envelope containing £500.00 was safely tucked into Max's designer suit inside pocket without affecting how the jacket draped from his shoulders. Max thought, ah see, get what you pay for; could have been a poacher's coat.

For all his bravado, Max couldn't entirely dispel a feeling of fear. There had been nothing to it. After all, he'd done nothing illegal. He'd just collected some worthless packaging and handed it to someone else. What was wrong with that? But the threat behind his initial illicit recruitment, the disappearance of his work predecessor, the confidence of the surly collection contact and the stark fact that he had become part of a pretty big-scale, hugely illegal narcotics operation all combined to make Max more scared than he could remember.

Safe in his secure flat, protected by hi-tech systems, Max poured a vodka and tonic and looked deep into himself. He knew that he shouldn't be doing what he was doing, but he also knew he'd been an easy recruit and that, given the same circumstances, he'd make the same decision again. As there was no going back, Max's thoughts redirected to wondering what would happen next. When would there be another consignment? When would he meet others from the conspiracy? Would Spray contact him directly? Was Spray behind all this?

There were no answers. Max had another drink, and alcohol induced confidence took control. Life is sweet as, he said to himself again, great flat, good job, nice car, chicks on tap and a monkey coming in, in cash, for doing fuck-all every so often – what's not to like? And as time progressed, Max's fear and occasionally guilty conscience dulled to a background mumble in his mind.

The weeks came and went, and the consignments came and went, in the same way, each time. Max's coffers grew fatter, and his insouciance at his actions and their possible – no, certain – effects grew too. Not my fault if people get hooked, he thought by way of self-justification, loads of people do coke all the time; no one gets hurt.

Max had settled into Onetelcall too. Apart from his covert activity, which demanded little time or effort, Max was good at his job, efficient and popular; he was a good organiser and a good manager. He had developed an easy relationship with his colleagues and a professional, even friendly rapport with Dan, his boss. Max admired Dan; he knew how well Dan had done to achieve his qualifications and to make the European arm of Onetelcall the growing success it was. Max harboured ambition in the company and realised that Dan was his passport to future success.

Dan wasn't so sure. He recognised in Max characteristics that he'd fought hard to defeat in himself. Greed, arrogance, slight immorality, variable integrity; all, perhaps, necessary in limited amounts but extremely dangerous when allowed untrammelled indulgence.

As Jo's court case got closer, Dan had to make some adjustments to allow for his time away from work. He called Spray to discuss.

"So that's it in a nutshell, Spray," said Dan long distance. "I'll be in court with Jo for at least three days and will probably have the day before and the day after off too."

"No problemo bub," replied Spray being irritatingly hip, "you know you gotta do what you gotta do and I'm right there behind you for sure. What you got planned?"

"Actually, timing is pretty good. We've got the Europe end of the tyre company contract sorted here and in Dordrecht. Karl in Strasbourg is on the case too. As far as management of the UK operation goes, well, it's only five days at the most and I thought I'd get young Max to cover. He's shown some promise and a bit of a challenge now might do him good."

"That the kid I met at the FalAk do in Amsterdam, right?"

"Yep, that's him. I took him on after your recommendation if you remember?"

"Yeah, sure. Look, Dan, give the kid my cell, right? If he has any issues, he can call me, Ok? That way, he'll feel supported, you needn't worry, and I'll know what's going on. Makes sense, eh? As I said a while ago, I've been thinking about coming over anyway, might time it for the end of your ordeal so we can celebrate a famous courtroom victory, whaddya say?"

"Thanks, Spray, that'd be great and thanks for the vote of confidence too. It does make sense, and I'll be grateful not to have to worry about work as well as Jo during the trial. It will be a night to remember when Jo's free and clear, but God knows what will happen if it goes the wrong way."

After the call, Dan invited Max into his office. He hadn't wanted to share any of the Jo story with anyone at work but felt Max should have an explanation as to why he'd have to take on a lot of responsibility for a short time.

"So, you see, Max," said Dan after giving him an outline sketch of the story so far, "you'll be me for about a week. Think you can handle it?"

Max looked like a puppy being given a doggy treat. Dan couldn't help but smile.

"I can see you think you can."

"I'm so grateful to you Dan. This is just great. I'll show you you're right to trust me, don't you worry, I'll be all over it."

"I know you will, Max, but just in case you get tripped up, here is Spray Wilson's cell number. He asked me to give it to you and he'll be there for you if you need him. For God's sake, call him instead of going it alone and making a mistake, Ok?"

Max's face paled. Dan couldn't know why.

"That's not a lack of faith in you Max, just a longstop, a safety measure to support you in my absence. Ok?"

Recovering from a sudden jolt of apprehension, Max said, "Oh yes, I understand and appreciate it. It's just that Spray may be a mate to you, but he's almost a deity to me, even more than you are… not to be blowing smoke at you… and it's a lot to take in, to know I can just call him if I need to, great though, thanks, really."

"Just keep an eye on things, Max. I'm not going to say any more now but just be aware of what's happening in the works. Something's going on, that's certain, and I think it may be that drugs are finding their way into the company. So, keep sharp and note anything that looks wrong to you."

Dan hadn't intended to mention drugs, but if Max could be trusted with the daily running of the business, then, thought Dan, he should be trusted with his concerns.

"No way," said Max with surprising fervour. "Drugs in Onetelcall? No way. Really? Why d'you think that? That's terrible. What drugs, I mean who, well, how? Crikey, I can't believe it, I've not seen anything."

"Steady on Max, no need to get too excited. It's nothing that affects the company's smooth running and, as far as I can see, everyone is working at a good speed with few errors, so no great worry, it might just be me being overly suspicious, I don't know."

It took until his journey home that evening for Dan to feel a sense of disquiet. Playing racing drivers in his 450 brake horsepower BMW was good for clarity of thinking for Dan. Concentration on the road cleared his mind and, as he slowed, his thoughts tended to drift back in order of priority.

Lifting off the throttle as he reached the turning home, Dan's thoughts found themselves wondering about Max. For one, Dan would have put money on Max being an occasional smoker-toker and probably a coke taker too. His reaction of shock and outrage at the suggestion of drugs on the company seemed a little excessive. And then, what about Max's reaction to the news that he could call Spray if he needed to? Deity? Dan knew the story about Spray and Max's meeting and what followed. In that brief time, Max had probably become closer to Spray than many ever did. Now, to Dan, Max's reaction looked odd. It looked like he was concealing something altogether different.

But what?

And then, a random thought muscled its way into Dan's consciousness. Spray had suggested taking a trip to Europe, but why would Max's short-term elevation to senior management become a sudden spur to come to England?

Surely not?

Christ, thought Dan, I'm turning into bloody Agatha Christie again. There is no great subterfuge and I'm no Hercule Poirot.

Taking stock as he parked, Dan mentally listed the attack on him, the attack on Jo, the suspicion of drugs coming into Onetelcall, doubt now about Max and even a passing question mark over Spray. Perhaps, thought Dan, I'd actually better get more Poirot-like and do it soon.

14

"It's nothing like the telly," beamed Simon as he strode up to Dan and Jo in the once-grand central hall of the Crown court building. The barrister's Raphael-like renaissance looks seemed oddly in place in the Baroque surrounding of the former Shire Hall. Completed in the mid-1800s and surrounded by more traditional Victorian brick architecture, the porticoed façade and Doric columns stood out proudly, their imposing elegance emphasising the building's importance. To walk through its black and gilded iron gates and up its stone steps to the main entrance was to feel intimidated, even more so when a gruff instruction to place any metal items in a tray came from security guards who treated everyone as a criminal, robe or not.

Once inside, the ambience was that of an unmodernised old state school. Staff, partly uniformed and heavily lanyarded, had all got something much more important to do than be of any assistance to the lost and bewildered visitors. Small groups of people stared vacantly at the unhelpful signs and notices, which were more about diversity policies than information or direction. How a great hall, once so beautiful, could be so degraded by the unstructured fly posting of semi-political notices and the unchecked indifference of those who worked and cared for it was a mystery to Dan.

They walked past the entrance to the barristers' robing rooms, past the café for commoners and into the lift, coffee-stained of course, to the second floor where Court 4 and Jo's destiny would be found. Still in original wood and marble, the court's outer hall offered only a few utilitarian seats and one low, stained table. Smartly dressed men and women rushed past, clutching laptops and mobile phones. Less smartly dressed men and women rushed a little slower and carried only clipboards and pads. Divides existed; roles were played. Dan tried and failed to suppress chuckles as self-importance paraded itself before him.

LED screens identifying the courtrooms shone out in the central foyer. The screens also announced the defendant's name, the judge who would preside and when. On either side of each court entrance were anterooms where barristers and defendants met for last-gasp discussion and preparation. Witnesses were not to be seen or spoken to here; they were a floor away, tended to by solicitors' assistants and court officials.

Simon was in a confident mood or, thought Jo, he was a particularly good actor. Jo felt reassured and not as undermined by fear as she had expected. A natural, fatalistic calm has settled on her. She and Simon were making conversation. He was expressing his readiness and she her optimism which was more hope than expectation.

Time moved at its slowest pace. Café machine coffee was at its most foul. Eventually, an usher unlocked the courtroom doors and, with a surprising amount of dignity, invited Jo to the dock.

Dan took his place in the visitors' area and gazed at his surroundings. Had he been expecting an impressive, pompous courtroom, he would have been disappointed. As a result, he thought, of a civil service interior design department, the courtroom was less a dignified auditorium and more a bland, functional, social services-style conference room. The only nod to the judge's status was an elevated judge's desk with large, high-backed, buttoned gloss leather and wood chairs behind it. One chair was larger than the others.

The chamber was the epitome of a lack of character. Pale oak, pale veneer and some birch-like laminates abounded and where there wasn't wood, there was pale cream paint, not brave enough to be magnolia.

Bullet-proof glass separated the accused from the rest. The defendant looked ahead to the bench, the jury to the left, the witness stand and a giant TV screen to the right. From the dock, Jo couldn't see Dan; he was seated in an area next to the dock on the right-hand side of the courtroom. Dan could see everything except Jo, which he found painful.

Both he and Jo could see the press desk, which had only one member of the fourth estate present. Am I getting old? Wondered Dan, as he speculated which newspaper this young man represented. Unfortunately, the reporter suffered from breakouts, or spots as Dan knew them; he also displayed long, lank and unpleasantly gleaming hair. Dan was not overly impressed but knew just what power that young man had.

Simon took his place in front and to the left of Jo, nearer to the jury. The prosecuting counsel took his position to the right of Simon and nearer to the witnesses. Dan wondered if there was any advantage as to who sat where but gave up in confusion. The clerk to the court, the recorder and the usher busily readied themselves for the hearing, scheduled to start at 10.00. At around 10.20, there was a loud knock on the wall at the very front of the room, and the clerk instructed everyone to stand.

The judge surprised Dan. She was attractive even in or perhaps because of her wig and gown. A younger person and a woman too thought Jo and Dan simultaneously; this had to be good. Dan had noted the prosecuting counsellor too. In contrast to the judge, the opposing QC was an older man with a red, whisky drinker's complexion and distended stomach. He looked like an old-time bellicose blusterer and courtroom bully.

Dan feared his cross-examination of Jo. Simon had warned Jo about the CPS's pet attack dog, Philip Peters QC, and Jo had assured him that she could take him on without any trepidation. "I've been beaten up by professionals," she assured him.

"Not by this professional you haven't," responded Simon. "He's a proud exponent of verbal pugilism; even his friends tread carefully when he's in full voice."

Preliminary business done with, it was time for the jury. Members filed in like self-conscious schoolchildren; the more mature ones looked very out of place. It was an even split, Dan noted, of men and women. There was also a representative spread of ages and an evident mix of ethnicity. Jo scanned the jury members and reflected that she probably couldn't have asked for a more unbiased selection. There were a couple of younger women who should be on her side almost regardless of evidence and a couple of 'old boys' who may have more archaic views about women wielding knives. Two other women had careworn looks. Jo wondered if they were oppressed by their menfolk, which could be good for her. A couple of the younger men were more interested in looking at the younger women and the judge. Jo had dressed to be demure, innocent and smart; she hoped she might appeal a little to these younger men too.

As the hearing got going, it all seemed mundane and slow to Dan. Lots of confirmations, re-readings, statements of facts, required legal statements and statutory declarations. The prosecution kicked off with some positioning about the dangers of knife attacks, attempted murders and other almost calumnious remarks. With both Simon and the judge interrupting him, the older QC ploughed on grinding his points into the jury's collective subconsciousness.

Police statements were read, and only one, Sgt Mick Cowan, Jo's chief interviewer and statement-taker, was called as a witness. The questioning was perfunctory from both sides.

Expert witness Dr Philip Drake came next. He confirmed the extent of the injury to Taylor. After the witness formalities, Dr Drake confirmed that Taylor had been seen in A&E and that he presented with a wound to his neck that measured 3cm wide and 2.6cm in depth. The wound, said Dr Drake, was immediately next to, but missing, the common carotid artery and required minor surgery to close it.

Philip Peters QC salivated like a man about to tuck into his favourite meal. "In your opinion, Dr Drake, could this stabbing have been fatal?" Short, succinct and punchy, Peters was pleased with his opening shot.

"In principle," replied Dr Drake in a careful monotone, "any cut to the common carotid artery could be lethal if not attended to; a severed artery will cause death in less than 30 seconds from excessive blood loss."

Peters appreciated the bonus point. "So, Mr Taylor is a lucky man to be here today?" That'll get the jury where it matters, he thought.

"Well, yes and no," responded Dr Drake. "The common carotid is about one and a half inches below the surface of the skin and quite difficult to sever. In Mr Taylor's case, the actual artery was not cut, and blood loss was consequently much less. It might have looked bloody and awful," Dr Drake paused while the jury appreciated his little wordplay, "but, as he was so quickly dealt with, his life was not, in fact, ever in danger."

If Peters could have harrumphed out loud, he would have done. "Are you suggesting then, Doctor Drake, that the knife missed its target, that the defendant Joanne Hadge failed to fatally stab her victim by a matter of mere, tiny millimetres?"

Keep banging away at those keywords, Peters told himself.

"I do not suggest, sir, I deal only in facts and medical findings. It is not for me to talk about intention. All I can say is what I've told you and I will say no more than that unless you have medically specific questions."

"Thank you for your candour, Doctor. I think we can all understand your professional position, no matter what your private thoughts may be. That will be all, thank you."

Simon stood up. "Just one question for you, Doctor, if I may. It is, of course, a question of fact and not mischievous speculation. From the angle of attack and entry, can you determine, medically and scientifically, if the wound was a passing blow or a direct strike?"

"Yes, I have seen many wounds like this, some obviously deliberate stabs, some attempts at suicide and some which were accidents. Stabs are notable because they are in a more direct line and result in a more even wound. A passing cut is more like a slice and shows a narrow-to-deep attitude that reveals sufficient force and directional information for us to form an informed opinion. In this case, I would say the wound was more consistent with a slice than a direct puncture and therefore more characteristic of a passing action rather than a direct stab."

Day one of the trial dragged on. There was a two-hour recess for lunch and other business for the judge, after which the prosecution case continued.

"So far today," began Philip Peters, addressing the jury, "we have had evidence from PCs Thomas and Pitt and also from the scene of crime investigator Ms Joiner, all of which indicates most powerfully that the defendant, Joanne Hadge, deliberately and viciously stabbed the hapless victim, Mr Kevin Taylor who was, as you will hear, answering what he thought was a plea for help from someone he knew, a friend, a very close friend."

Peters had avoided mentioning, noted Simon, evidence from PC Amanda Cotter, which, when read, had been more favourable to Jo.

"We have also heard from Dr Drake, who informed us, in his role as expert, that the defendant had been only a tiny fraction away from lethally stabbing the victim."

Simon stood up just as the judge spoke: "This isn't a summing up, Mr Peters, as you well know, and you are trying…."

Philip Peters held up his hands in faux surrender. "Of course, your honour, and I apologise, if I may, for my excessive zeal in wanting to put the case for the prosecution to the jury clearly and without obfuscation. I will if I may, your honour, now proceed with the next prosecution witness."

In her short time as a Crown Court judge, Jennifer Gordon QC had developed an authoritative dismissive, disdainful look, a look she now bestowed on Philip Peters. "You have been warned, Mr Peters, I do not give second warnings. Proceed by all means but proceed with care."

In preparing their case, the Crown Prosecution Service team had instructed Peter Philips to call a limited number of witnesses, basing selection on likelihood to impress a jury and thereby improve the chances of a conviction.

Peggy, they decided, was a better bet than the often-belligerent Eric. She had been extensively familiarised with the prosecution's position. Coaching a witness is, of course, frowned on but making them aware of all relevant circumstances is allowed. Eric had reminded his wife that their position in the town relied on their discretion, "Co-operate, talk a lot and tell 'em nothing, like you do," instructed Eric. Peggy understood; she was ready.

"Are you Peggy Woods, landlady of The Carpenters Arms?"

"Yes sir, I am with my hubby Eric. Well, he's not a landlady, he's a landlord, see what I mean?"

"Quite so. Tell me, Mrs Woods…."

"Oh, you can keep on calling me Peggy, dear."

"Indeed, thank you, Peggy. Tell me, Peggy, do you recognise the defendant in the dock?"

"Oh yes, dear, I know her, she's been in our lovely pub, you know, I remember her, she's so pretty, isn't she?"

"When the defendant was in your pub, was she on her own or was she in the company of other people?"

"Oh well, dear, now let me see. She's been in a few times I seem to remember. Always so nice and looking so pretty. I always remember the nice people. She's ever so friendly, isn't she, so I expect she'd have been chatting away with my regulars, they are a lovely bunch, my regulars, they always welcome everyone, especially the pretty girls, well, I mean, they would, wouldn't they, I mean, they are men after all, well, most of them, and men, well, they do, don't they, they do like a pretty girl."

"I see, yes, thank you, Mrs… Peggy… is there one of your regulars who you remember particularly talking to the defendant?"

"Well now, dear, let me see, yes, I think so. She seemed to know one of my best boys, we call him Sniff but I think his real name is Kevin Taylor. They seem to be friends if you know what

I mean?"

"Do you mean, Peggy, that you believe the defendant and Mr Taylor are friends and that you have seen them in friendly conversation together in your public house?"

"Well, yes, dear, that's what I said innit, she and our Sniff, laughing and chatting away, it's what our lovely little pub is for, isn't it, good friends meeting for a drink and a good time together."

Peter Philips wasn't brave enough to push it any further; he feared a slip of attention from the garrulous Peggy.

Judge Jennifer Gordon QC had had enough. She could see that the jury had had enough too. A day of two sessions of police statements, an expert and then the appalling Peggy was enough for anyone.

"We shall recess for the day now," announced Jennifer as Peggy's testimony came to an end. "This court will be in session tomorrow at 10.00 precisely."

"All stand."

Everyone stood, and the judge exited as gracefully as the narrow corridor between her chair and the door to her antechamber would allow.

The court emptied, and Dan and Jo met Simon in the foyer.

"What do you think," asked a nervous and strained-looking Jo.

"So far, so good," said Simon. "The prosecution is trying to establish a picture of you deliberately aiming at Taylor and will, no doubt, push a story that you know him, perhaps even imply that there is a reason why you'd want to hurt him. Tomorrow will be interesting. I don't think the jury is as gullible as the prosecution needs for a successful conviction."

Jo looked downhearted. "I thought the doctor did a good job for us, didn't you?"

Dan and Simon nodded in unison but more out of sympathy than certainty.

"Jo, I'm sure the trial will run for its full three days, but just in case, and I have to say this out of duty, not pessimism, you should pack some clothes and personal essentials, just in case of remand."

"Oh fuck," said Jo, tears smearing her make-up.

15

Max was having a blast. Karl called him from the Strasbourg office to offer any help and support he may need, and in Dordrecht, the local operations manager, his Dutch equivalent, Chloe sent an email from her home office asking Max to call her when he had a moment, which he did. The big tyre company contract was ahead of schedule and regional sales were increasing. Between them, Max, Chloe and Karl were on top of their games, and Max knew that Dan would be pleased.

Max told himself he deserved a drink and, unusually, stopped off at The Carpenters Arms. It was not his type of pub, but the draught bitter was excellent, and that's just what he fancied.

Duggie recognised 'Slicko' the moment he walked in. It was unusual for Duggie to be in 'Sniff's pub,' but he'd called in hoping to bump into his chum and mentor.

"A pint of your wonderful bitter please," Max asked of Eric, who responded with action, not word or smile. Eric was a master of taciturn.

Max looked around. His eye settled for an instant on Duggie and then moved on. I'm sure I know that little bloke, he thought as his mind drifted back to the clattering Ford Escort and his first illicit transaction in the Onetelcall car park.

Several poly bubble packs later, Max was more familiar with the car than its driver but seeing Duggie, even out of context, made the image clearer. Apart from a young couple sharing a bottle of wine at the window table and two middle-aged men leaning against the bar, heads close in earnest conversation, it was just Duggie and Max at the beer-taps end of the bar.

Max decided.

"Buy you a beer?"

Duggie was overwhelmed with confusion and unidentifiable foreboding. Should he say 'yes' or 'no'? Should he know Max or not? Should they be talking or not? What would Sniff say? Christ.

"Stella please."

Eric, unasked, obliged and placed Duggie's new pint down with a meaningful splosh. Duggie knew it was a meaningful gesture but had no idea what the meaning was.

"Cheers, thanks." God, don't let him talk to me, please make him go.

"Yeah, cheers. Quiet in here today, isn't it," commented Max to Duggie and Eric together.

"Oh yes," blurted Duggie, "court, you know, they're all in court."

Max's senses rang their alarm.

"Really?" he responded with one of his winning smiles, "all in court, eh? What on earth have they all done? Nothing too serious, I hope, no prison sentences in the offing, are they?" he said with a laugh in his voice.

"Ain't nothing to talk about," declared Eric, with taciturn factor turned up to eleven. "The wife's just a witness in some case involving one of our regulars, that's all. No one's done nothing wrong round here, and that's a fact."

Max nodded his understanding.

"Courts are tedious, long-winded affairs usually; your wife has my sympathy."

Duggie listened, watched and thought if Max and Eric were talking, he must be on safe ground, besides which he might get another pint out of 'Slicko.'

"Yeah, I've been in court, you know, it was fuckin pants. Loads of toffs in wigs playing God over normal folk like me. Arseholes."

"Always the way, isn't it? There's always someone who can

lord it over you," agreed Max, in his matiest way. "So, you probably know the chap in court then, do you?"

"Oh yeah," enthused Duggie, "he's my mate, he looks after me, and I do jobs for him. Sniff's a good chap, that's what he is. Anyway, he's a witness to you know, just like Peggy is, he's not been accused of nothing or nothing like that."

"That's Ok then. I'll bet they'll be pleased when they've been called, said their bit and got it over and done with. It messes your week up, waiting for your turn without knowing when it's going to be."

Max may have made some bad life decisions at times, but he was never slow to catch nuances, and he'd realised quickly that the case in which Peggy and Sniff were witnesses would be the case of his boss's girlfriend being accused of GBH. Max tried to make sense of it all. He knew Duggie worked for Sniff, which meant Sniff must be the reseller of the cocaine coming into Onetelcall in those poly bubble bags. He guessed Peggy would be in court saying whatever Sniff had told her to say, but what? Why had Sniff attacked Dan's girlfriend? Was it drugs? Was it sex? What?

Max picked up his pint and peered at Duggie over the mug's rim. He saw a man approaching middle age with little to show for his years. He saw nervousness and doubt; he saw vague desperation, a misfit trying oh so hard to fit in. Max reckoned he had the measure of Duggie and felt a background flicker of sympathy for the man who was evidently Sniff's stooge, delivery driver and Max had no doubt, fall-guy for Sniff if or when things went wrong.

Max decided to take a risk.

"Max, by the way," said Max as an introduction, "you are…?

"I'm Duggie." Anxiety flashed visibly across Duggie's pale features.

"Ok, Duggie, good to say hello properly," Max's voice carried the intended implication.

Duggie smiled feebly, his anxiety deepening.

"This court case then, Duggie, it'll be the one about your chum Sniff being stabbed, I expect?"

Duggie felt trapped but resolved to speak bravely.

"Yeah, that's the one. Very nearly got killed did Sniff; we all reckon the girl what stabbed him should be put away, locked up for being a bloody nutter."

"I've met her," said Max, now holding Duggie's eyes like a lamper, "she seemed very nice to me, no signs of being a nutter at all; she's my boss's girlfriend actually, so he's in court too, holding her hand so to speak, but I expect you knew that didn't you?"

Oh shit, thought Duggie, wondering what he should say next.

"Sort of," he muttered.

"Yeah, you know a lot, don't you, Duggie. Much more than you want to talk about, isn't that right? In fact, we both know a lot, don't we, Duggie? In fact, we are in similar positions, you and I, aren't we?"

"Whaddya mean, what are you saying?"

"I'm just saying, we both know the main people in this trial, that's all, we both work for people in the trial one way or another, don't we? What else could I be saying?"

Duggie stared at Max without replying.

Max finished his pint and walked quickly towards Duggie. Eric moved closer to keep an eye and ear on this unexpected development, but Max was too sudden for his less-than-nimble, lumbering frame.

"Here," said Max, pushing, unseen by Eric, his business card into Duggie's coat pocket. "That's me, and I've got a feeling you might need me one day; you might need someone to help you. Call me when that happens, OK? Just nod, don't speak."

Duggie nodded as Max walked away. To Eric, it looked like a

goodbye nod. To Duggie, it was a nod of relief, gratitude and, most of all, hope.

Max relaxed a little as he settled into the sculptured-squab seat in his Audi S3. As he drove the couple of miles back to his converted farm-building flat, he forced himself to consider his position again. He admitted to himself that morality was not his strong suit; he knew he had hedonistic tendencies and a fondness for the sybaritic. Taking £500 in cash, for every consignment of what he knew, pretty certainly, to be cocaine didn't trouble his conscience too much. Given a status quo, he'd go on in the same way, but somehow, he knew circumstances were shifting from essentially harmless – if you didn't think about the catastrophic effects of coke on its users, that is – to potentially very dodgy indeed.

He was sure that Sniff bullied the weak and pliant Duggie into doing his risky work. He knew that Dan had suspicions about drugs coming into Onetelcall, and he would bet his car and watch, his most valued possessions, that CEO Spray Wilson was the 'capo di tutti capi' in this surreal drama.

Max knew one fact he couldn't and wouldn't duck; he wasn't going to see Dan get caught up in anything drug orientated. He could see how it might happen. Dan trusts people, he said to himself. He trusts me, and he obviously trusts Spray. If we wanted to, we could make Dan carry the can for the whole shebang, and Dan wouldn't have a leg to stand on. Even this trial suggests that Dan could be implicated with Sniff; he could be dead meat so easily.

Max had another thought. Dan had trusted him enough to share his fears of drugs coming into the company. What if, pondered Max, Dan was doing some sleuthing of his own? What if he was trying to get to the bottom of the drugs business and cut it out?

"Fuck," said Max out loud to himself. It was an unbearable thought.

Max parked his beloved car and let himself into his indulgent home. He heard a movement. He saw a shape. There was someone in his flat.

"Hi Max, how's tricks? Just come a-checkin' on ya'll."

16

Day two and at 10.00 precisely, the assembled court awaited the next instalment of Jo's trial. At a less-than-precise 10.23, the now-familiar sound of wall-knocking heralded the judge's imminent entrance.

The first session, and possibly the second, would be for Peter Philips QC to complete his case for the prosecution. After the usual courtly preambles and notices, he looked at the jury and began,

"Yesterday, we heard sworn statements from police officers, a scene of crime expert and heard the testimony of an expert witness, Doctor Drake, and then a most informative witness, Peggy Wood, established the relationship between the victim and the accused."

Peter Philips paused, knowing he was about to be censured again. He looked at the judge in unspoken apology and, from her seat on high, Jennifer Gordon silently tutted and gave the prosecuting council a nod to continue.

"Today, we will hear from witnesses who will provide all the information I know you are wanting, all the questions you have will be answered, and we shall also hear from the victim himself."

Simon jumped to his feet. Peter Philips sat down.

The judge said, "This isn't a TV show, Mr Philips, we do not need a build-up, and we do not need a review from you. The jury will note that no establishment of a relationship has been proven. It will be for you, the jury, and not Mr Philips to decide that matter of victimisation. We will proceed, Mr Philips, but remember this is a court of law and will be treated with the utmost respect."

"Your honour, no one has more respect for the courts of this land than I," bowed the artful QC. "I shall indeed proceed to enable the jury to reach the right decision, and I shall call Susan Clark, witness as listed in your bundle A, your honour and ladies and gentlemen."

Susan Clark had worked with Jo at the IT Consultancy, Raglan Inc. when Jo had been an in-house events specialist. Jo was surprised and disturbed when she saw, in her pre-trial CPS file, that Susan would be called as a prosecution witness. Susan was dressed in a dark blue suit, a white open-necked shirt set off with a thin pearl choker. Her dark hair was formal in a careful ponytail. Professional and, therefore, plausible, thought Jo. Had they been able to comment, the jury would have agreed.

Peter Philips established Susan's name, details and occupation, that she and Joanne Hadge had worked for Raglan Inc. together and knew Joanne Hadge well. In answer to questioning, Susan told the court,

"Yes, I do remember seeing Jo and the man I now know to be Kevin Taylor together. It was at one of our company events at The Royal George Hotel. Mr Taylor seemed very familiar with Jo and had some nickname for her which I cannot now recall."

"So, you would say they, that being the defendant and Mr Taylor, knew each other and possibly had some sort of relationship?" asked Philips, hoping he hadn't pushed too far.

"I would say," replied Susan carefully, her eyes moving slowly from the prosecutor to Jo and back again, "that she did know Mr Taylor, but I wouldn't say they had any relationship as such. I do remember that Jo didn't seem to like Mr Taylor very much and, if I may say, I think she referred to him as a slimeball."

Sod it, thought Philips, who had feared such a comment. He knew he shouldn't have given the witness such an easy opportunity, he was better than that. He moved on with a positivity he didn't feel.

"You can remember her name for him but not his nickname for her, I see. You were a good close friend of Ms Hadge, weren't you? Close enough, I'm sure, to be loyal and protective. Most laudable as long as it doesn't interfere with the real truth, which is that the defendant and the victim, Mr Taylor, were at a company event together, they spent time together, they knew each other and, as we have heard, they were known to laugh together and evidently enjoy themselves together, isn't that right Ms Clark?"

"You must think what you want; all I can say is what I know. And what I know is…."

"Yes, thank you, Ms Clark, we have heard your evidence, and I won't ask you to repeat it all again, thank you."

Simon had no questions.

Peter Philips also called James Ansell, General Manager at The Royal George. Dapper and confident, Ansell spoke to the prosecutor and to the jury as he confirmed that he, too, had seen Jo and Taylor in conversation at the Raglan event and that they appeared to know each other. He had not heard Jo make any comments or express any opinion about Taylor and couldn't say if the two seemed to have a relationship.

Next in the witness box was John Mayhew, manager at the Biggabookie betting office where Jo had withdrawn money from the shop's ATM and had seen Taylor as she left. Mayhew interested the jury because he was a completely independent witness with evidence about one of the greyer areas of Jo's defence.

Jo believed that Sniff had followed her back to her flat from Biggabookie, and that was how he might know where she lived. The police hadn't concerned themselves with this as they did not believe that how her address was known to Taylor was relevant to the attack. Simon had suggested to Dan and Jo that he might be able to make it relevant but would let the prosecuting counsellor call Mayhew as his witness to see where his evidence would go.

"I am John Mayhew, manager at the Olderbury branch of Biggabookie, and yes, I do remember seeing the defendant in my shop; we don't get very many customers like her and, to be fair, she was, well, is, more memorable than most of my customers, so yes, I do. She didn't place a bet. She came in and used the ATM in our foyer; it's there so my customers can have ready access to cash to bet with."

Some of the jury members allowed themselves an audible snigger.

"I'm sorry, I can't remember who she talked to apart from her saying 'hello' to another of my customers who I call 'Sniff,' but he's properly called Kevin, I believe. No, I can't say if they had a long conversation, but, yes, they did seem matey to me."

Satisfied he'd shown the jury another example of Jo and Taylor having some form of friendship, Peter Philips handed his witness over to Simon for cross-questioning. This time Simon did have a question, and he asked it.

"As it happens, I did see her leave. Not that I was watching her or anything, I just noticed. Well, you do, don't you," he looked at the jury and some of the male members nodded.

Simon watched this little interplay with interest and noted it for later. Then he asked what might be a crucial question for the defence,

"Did you see anyone follow the defendant when she left your premises?"

"I believe so, sir, yes. I'm pretty sure someone left as soon as she did. I happened to notice through our front window as she walked past, a chap was leaving my shop at the same time."

"So, you were watching quite closely. Did you notice who it was?"

"Well, to be honest, I noticed her more than him, not that I was watching especially, you know, just happened to notice as you do. Well, though, now I think about it, I'm almost certain, well I think it might have been Sniff – only I think it was him 'cos I remember wondering if was going to, you know, give her a bit chat and that."

John Mayhew had given a good performance, he thought. He'd been worried as hell about being called as a witness but decided to cooperate as being a prosecution witness meant he'd be on Sniff's side. Being on Sniff's side was important as Sniff supplied all Mayhew's coke. Mayhew made good money from this side-line and kept himself 'happy' too; he didn't want to rock the boat – or get beaten up.

Peter Philips addressed the court,

"I had scheduled to call Mr Tom Alderton at this point. Mr Alderton was, in effect, the first responder when Mr Taylor had been stabbed."

Simon stood up again but, seeing the momentum was passing, sat down again. He heard Jo's hiss of annoyance.

"I think, however, the jury has full information about the wound inflicted on Mr Taylor, and we need not take up any more of the court's valuable time on the matter. Mr Alderton would also have corroborating evidence, which is still available to the court if needed, about Mr Taylor's condition, physically and mentally, immediately after the attack, when he sought assistance in The Coopers Arms. However, no one can give better evidence of this than the victim himself, so I now call Kevin Taylor."

Simon was not surprised by this change in the running order, and he knew why. Tom Alderton had one piece of evidence the CPS had, it seemed, tried to hide.

The doors opened, and the witness assistant and the court usher accompanied Taylor to the witness box. Taylor leant on the usher's arm; the witness assistant guided him by the shoulder.

Thank you, God, said Dan to himself, thank you for delivering him pissed; it might just save Jo from prison.

Peter Philips looked at his leading player in what he secretly thought was a CPS farce. He could see Taylor was wobbly, and he knew that the judge could easily hold him contempt if he were inebriated. In pre-trial meetings, Peter Philips had warned him not to drink or ingest any substances. "Don't worry, fella,"

Taylor had said, "I'll just say I'm handicapped, that always works." Philips had only just contained his expression of disgust.

Taylor took the oath and steadied himself against the witness box railings; through his favourite gold-framed specs, he peered at the prosecuting counsel. After confirming, as requested, his name, age, address and details, Kevin 'Sniff' Taylor leaned against the top rail of the witness box and gazed expectantly at the prosecuting barrister with a conspiratorial, knowing grin.

"Mr Taylor,"

"Yes, mate."

Peter Philips stifled a grimace and noticed that the jury members were looking hard-faced and probably a little unimpressed.

"Mr Taylor, are you feeling well enough to give evidence?"

"Oh yes mate, just got a bit of an ache in me back and leg, old injuries, you know, give me a bit of gip they do."

Philips doubted even Sniff's mother would have believed him, but it was better than nothing and the jury looked slightly mollified.

"Good, thank you, Mr Taylor."

"Orlrite mate."

"Mr Taylor, this is, as you know, a formal court, so shall we proceed now with all due respect?"

Sniff's slouching attitude became a little more upright, and he moved his arms from the railing to let his hands rest by his sides.

"Yes sir," without any obvious sarcasm or acknowledgement of being rebuked.

"Good, thank you. Now, Mr Taylor. I think it would help you and help the jury too if we start with events which are alleged to have happened before the night of your stabbing."

"OK with me,"

Philips asked Sniff about seeing Jo in Biggabookie. Sniff confirmed that he had. Had he followed her from the shop to her home to ascertain her address?

"No mate, no need for all that following malarkey, me and Jo, well, we're tight if you know what I mean, she'd given me her address and phone number ages ago; known her for some time, haven't I."

"Have you indeed, Mr Taylor, how long would you say you've known the defendant?"

"Bloody ages, sorry, bloomin' ages now innit. She and me's tight, and that's how it's been for a long time."

"Would you say that you had a good relationship with the defendant? We have heard that the defendant wasn't very friendly when you met at The Royal George, for instance?"

"Oh yeah, I mean, we've been a bit more than friendly, if you follow my drift. I've known Jo-Jo, that's what I call her, see, Jo Jo, an' Arizona Grass, that's another of my names for her – Beatles an' that, Get Back Jo Jo innit, and you know, Jo Jo she's been round my gaff an' that for, well, you know, what you call relations, know what I mean, dripping for it she was, me and Jo Jo was sweet enough…"

Peter Philips interrupted,

"You are telling the court, Mr Taylor, that you and the defendant were more than just friends and that, in fact, you and she had had a sexual relationship. Is that correct, Mr Taylor?"

"Fucking' right, mate…"

"Mr Taylor," Judge Jennifer could tolerate no more, "I will hold you in contempt of court if you use such unacceptable language."

She turned her attention to the agitated-looking counsellor, "Mr Phillips, please take control of your witness if you wish this trial to continue. I will have no hesitation in terminating proceedings if there is any more obvious contempt. Do you understand, do both of you understand?"

"Your honour, I apologise to you and everyone in this court, and I am sure Mr Taylor will apologise too."

"Yeah, sorry your judge," Sniff followed the QC's lead, "it's just how I talk, you know, didn't mean to, you know, piss …offend anyone," Sniff gave an audible hiccup in conclusion.

"Mr Taylor, I have to ask if you have been drinking, have you consumed any alcohol or any other mind-affecting substance before appearing in this court?"

"Well, miss, I had to have a pint or two, it's for the pain in me back, see, a pint or two takes the edge off, doesn't it?"

The judge said nothing further; she nodded at Philips, who took her unspoken cue.

"Mr Taylor, can I have your assurance that you are fully aware of what you are saying and that you are not, at all, confused or in any state of disabling intoxication?"

"You're alright, sir, I'm not pi… under any influence, course I'm not, I'm used to it anyway aren't I, never lose control, that's me."

Peter Philips noticed again how unimpressed the jury looked.

"Let's us continue, shall we, Mr Taylor? To recap for the jury, can you confirm that you have been on friendly terms with the defendant for some appreciable length of time and that you have had a sexual relationship with her in the past?"

"S'right, that is."

"Can I also confirm that you tell us that the defendant had given you her address and telephone number at some time before you ran into her in Biggabookie?"

"That's it, chief, yeah, that's how it is right enough, me and Jo Jo, that's why I was at her place when the bitch bloody stabbed me."

"Mr Taylor," the judge used her most stern look and voice,

"I've warned you once, and you have chosen to ignore my warning."

"Mr Philips," the judge's glare lit on Peter Philip's reddening face. "I am minded to dismiss this case. If it weren't such a serious charge that may involve a custodial sentence, I would have no hesitation. Do you understand? However, I shall allow you to continue but be very certain that you must ensure the appropriate behaviour and language from your client who, I'm sure, understands the consequences of any further failure to heed my words."

"Your honour, I am most grateful for your forbearance, and I am sure my client is equally in your debt. This is, as you say, a serious matter, and my client, as the prosecution case argues, is the victim who has a special interest in seeing justice being done today."

Sniff, his arms on the witness box railings again tried his best to look apologetic but managed only an expression of comic ruefulness.

"Let us carry on, Mr Taylor, and keep in the uppermost of your mind that this is, as I said, a court of law which demands your full respect. Is that understood, Mr Taylor?"

"Yes, sir," Sniff with feigned dignified contrition.

Peter Philips took a deep breath, adjusted his wig and made a wing shape with the drapes of his gown. This is it, he thought, if I'm going to get a prosecution, I've got to get a performance out of that slob in the box. Here goes,

"Tell me, Mr Taylor…"

17

"Christ's sake, Spray, Mr Wilson, how did you get in here? I'm supposed to be safe as a bug in a civil service computer here!"

Spray grinned. His young mule had nerve.

"Cinch, but you gotta figure it for yourself, but let me tell ya, if it's got a chip, I can hack it."

"Drink?"

"Sure, gotta bourbon?"

"In Olderbury? How about a proper whisky, one that comes from Scotland?"

Max poured the drinks and, feeling he needed some acquired status, perched on his high bar-style stool to look downwards at his night visitor.

"Whaddya say then, Max? You getting along, Ok? I hear good things about ya at work, the boys in Europe rate ya and how you've backed-up Dan, good work, man, good work."

"Thanks," said Max, his thoughts cartwheeling, "it's been a blast, and Dan is such a good leader that all I had to do was what I thought he'd do, and sometimes a bit of what I thought I should do too."

"Yeah, cool. But you'll guess that I'm not here now to talk shop, I'm here to talk about our particular kind of shopping and, before you think about it, I've already swept your pad for any listeners; all your AI stuff is temporarily indisposed, right?"

"I see," said Max, his sangfroid wavering.

"Yeah, well, here it is Max, I kinda get a feeling that Dan, for sure one of the world's really good guys, is getting just a bit hinky about gear getting into his works; whaddya reckon, eh Max, what's the word?"

Max, tensing inside, tried to look calm and knowing. He had to take a position that he could sustain and that wouldn't end up with him or Dan 'disappearing' like his predecessor.

"Truth of the matter is Spray," said Max regretting it as he said it, only people about to fib start with a declaration of honesty, "Dan's been so up to his neck in his girlfriend's terrible ordeal and now her trial that we haven't talked much about anything other than what I would have to do for him and the business while he was away. Other than that, it's all easy. Stuff comes in, stuff goes out and no one in the works, or anywhere else, notices anything they shouldn't; it all goes like clockwork."

"Good to hear, man, good to hear. But I've got a feeling that things are getting a lot more complex with this business about Dan's girl Jo being accused of attacking a dude here in Olderbury who, and this is for you only, better know what I mean, might be connected with the stuff you handle in the warehouse, y'see?"

Max looked calmer than he felt. "Like I said, Dan and I didn't talk about Jo's troubles much, and I don't know the ins and outs of it all or who is supposed to have done what. I know she stabbed a guy who has a pretty dodgy reputation around here, that would be who you are referring to, I suppose, but I can't say I know him, I only know by sight the chap who drives a tatty old Ford and who collects the stuff from me and gives me, well, you know, my envelope."

"Ok, Max, but I gotta tell ya, I got one of them deep down cold feelings like heavy shit is about to fall from the skies and land all over me and that ain't gonna happen while I still call the shots."

"So that's why you are here now, like this," said Max, realising that Spray meant business.

"For sure. The way I see it, Dan could find out that the man his girl stabbed is a dealer. He might decide to find out if he's the dealer who's feeding C into his plant. I know he's already done a trial score, and he'll keep on digging; he's that sort of guy, clever, determined and straight. Other ways around, the dealer, who calls himself Sniff for fuck's sake, might well decide to get at Dan by doing something dickhead like pushing more dope into the company or by threatening Dan that he'll go to the feds with a frame on Dan… you see, the risks are many and varied, and all of them put me in danger and that, as I said, ain't going to happen.

"And while we are talking of who is in danger, I'm here to tell you that you are in a helluva bind too, 'cos if I'm at risk, then so are you, and I mean big time. Be sure of this, I'll be your buddy for as long as everything is cool, but if I go down, I ain't going alone, so you'd better be the best bodyguard you can be if we are going to get through this, you got me?"

Max needed time to think. He took Spray's glass and walked slowly to his drinks shelf. A long stream of Scotch, a splash of water and, for his American visitor, the requisite ice. Max looked back over his shoulder to say,

"I'm not sure I fully understand Spray. I mean, I can see the possible risks as you describe them, although I'm not sure just how real those risks are yet; even if any of the circumstances you think might happen actually do happen, what is it that you think I can or should do? My only role is an intermediary, a go-between, I don't have any influence over Dan or this Sniff of yours."

For the first time, Max was struck by the emptiness in Spray's eyes. He was unnerved.

"Oh man, you gotta know life ain't that simple. When I met you in Holland, you wanted me to know how worldly you were, said you'd been around, that you knew the score, you could look after yourself, so don't come the innocent now. You handle illegals, you become illegal and all that goes with it. You got me?"

"So far Spray, so far…"

"Cool, 'cos here's the thing. When the cracks appear, you gotta act, you gotta smooth them over, you gotta keep me safe, 'cos that way you keep you safe. You know it, yeah?"

"Come on, Spray," said Max showing a confidence he didn't feel, "spell it out for me; I don't want to misunderstand you."

"Oh, you'll understand me, no mistake. Way I see it, either Dan or the Sniff dude will become dangerous. Don't know which yet. Maybe both, who knows what's going to unwrap? You Max? You're going to watch what happens closer than a mummy eagle watches her chicks, you got me? You're going to keep me posted on everything, and I mean everything that happens, important or not. And, for the avoidance of any doubt, as my lawyers keep on saying, if those deep cracks appear and you can't smooth them over, we'll make them disappear. And I know you know what I mean. I've got resources, human resources who do what I ask. I pay them well to do whatever I ask. You follow? They make difficulties vanish. Keep me safe, keep you safe, I'll provide the how you provide the information and the opportunity for my boys' style of active management. OK?"

Max almost smiled at Spray's illusory expressions. Just like a streamed B movie. Except, he was not in the cast of baddies. His look must have given his thoughts away.

"I can see it in your face, Max. You ain't about to have anything to do with anything heavy, right? You don't want to know about problems being vanished, about dudes who do things, about making arrangements that will have consequences you can't even imagine. Yeah? You gotta life, it's easy, you get money without feeling guilty, you hide from your mind that you are knowingly peddling snow and all that means. You are a little boy playing in a big boy's playground, and now you gotta grow up real fast. You gotta know playtime means pay time. 'Cos if you decide to run away, you just check out the guy who did your job before you. You'll look for him. You won't find him. He don't exist no more. He's vapourware. That's what happens to guys who don't play the game like grown-ups. You got me, Max? You solid?"

"Oh yes, I've got you, Spray. And as we are putting our cards on the table and because we've got to trust each other more than ever now, I'll be candid and straightforward. You know it, Spray, I'm no hard man, I don't do violence, I don't know how to. But I am loyal, and that's my only problem, one I think we share. I couldn't do anything which would hurt Dan, OK? I've got to say that now, so you know. I don't give a stuff about your Sniff chap, but if it is Dan who becomes one of your cracks that needs smoothing, we'd have to find a cleverer way than resorting to muscle-bound gun-totin' human resources."

Spray smiled again and Max, for the first time since he'd seen Spray sitting in his Layzeeboy, relaxed.

"I knew I'd got you right. You're a smart son-of-a-bitch. You ain't in no position to bargain, and yet, here you are, telling me what you will and won't do. I've had men broken for less. But you have made a point I can't argue. Most people, well, I don't care about them, but Dan is a special case, and he is a friend, one of the very few I've ever had. He matters to me too. If he's a problem, we'll find a way around it without him knowing. Ok? Satisfy your British sensitivity, you goddam limey."

Max nodded in agreement, wondering if Spray was as good as his word. Was Dan a particular case to be protected, or would Spray take the final sanction and, perhaps, what happens to Dan would happen to him too?

18

Dan could feel the tension, the anticipation. The jury was waiting for the prosecution to make its case. The man in the witness box was the crucial witness. Prosecutor Peter Philips rose to his moment, as he had done for so many years before.

"Tell me, Mr Taylor, tell the jury exactly why you knocked on the door of the defendant's flat in the early hours of that morning?"

Sniff stood up straight and aimed his gaze at the jury.

"Well, I could hear her, couldn't I? I could hear her shouting like she was in trouble or something. Well, it's me innit, I wanted to help her didn't I, so, with her shouting a lot an' that, I knocked on her door, see, I mean, I'd help her if she needed me to, that's all it was, I just wanted to, you know, be a good mate and weigh-in for her."

"I see; you heard her shouting and were worried for her well-being, is that correct?"

"Yeah, that's it, chief, sir."

"Can you describe for the court exactly how events of that night unfolded, step by step, what happened?"

Sniff selected one of his more arrogant, slightly cocky looks from his menu of facial expressions and fixed the jury, not his questioner, with a half-smile of familiarity.

"It went, I was walking home, goin' past The Coopers when I could see the lights in Jo-Jo's flat was on and I could hear screaming and shouting. Well, I thought something's up here, and I couldn't walk by if my old booty-girl was in trouble, so I went up to her door and banged on it.

"She come down, doesn't she, after a while, she come down and opens the door. I says to her, 'you Ok darlin,' you want any help an' that? Well, she opened the door right wide, and I thought to myself, she wants me to go in, so I went to go in and, bosh, she come at me wiv a fuc… wiv a bloody great knife, pointed straight at me 'ead it was. Fuck me, I thought, the cow's goin' to fuckin' stab me. Well, I dodged a bit, didn't I? Well, you would, wouldn't you, but whammo, she only stuck right in my bloody neck, didn't she? Right in my bloody neck, right here," Sniff paused to indicate his still visible scar, "see it? You can see it, can't you? No bloody doubt about that, is there? Stabbed in the neck I was, and I was only trying to help.

"And then, well, I couldn't believe that I'd been, like, stabbed, you know and then, what happened, eh? I'll tell you what, the next thing I know is that Jo-Jo was coming at me again, waving her fist at me she was and then she only bloody smashed me in the face with her other hand didn't she, thumped she did, bloody thumped me…"

Sniff allowed his body to subside into a slouch against the witness box rail, the epitome of nervous exhaustion from the effort of reliving his ordeal.

"Thank you, Mr Taylor, I think the jury now has a clear understanding of the events as they unfolded but, if I may, can I just confirm that you were walking past, saw lights, heard screams, knocked on the door out of concern for the well-being of a friend. When the door was opened by the defendant, instead of being welcomed, you were attacked and stabbed, deliberately stabbed in the neck and then physically assaulted by way of being struck in the face by the defendant's deliberately balled fist; is that all correct?"

Peter Philips made a fist and showed it to the jury as a visual amplification.

"Yeah, that's what happened right enough, it was her." Sniff pointed his finger at the dock, "it was her, stabbed me she did, and she meant it too."

Peter Philips was satisfied. Taylor had made most of the key points he had been asked to make to give the CPS any chance of achieving its prosecution for the charges it had levelled at Joanne Hadge. The 'with intent' aspect added a significant layer of seriousness to the case, and Taylor had suitably emphasised that necessary point. He pressed on,

"Tell the court please, Mr Taylor, what did you do next?"

Sniff continued his dramatic discourse. He explained how he staggered to the pub and was eventually let in. He described his pain and bloodied state, how the off-duty ambulance man had tended to him, how he'd been taken to hospital and treated, with 'an operation' before being released.

Philips, not one to miss a chance to emphasise key points, said,

"May I put it this way, Mr Taylor, for clarification for the jury, you were in fear for your very life when you found refuge in a close-by pub and were saved, in effect, by the ministrations of a medical professional who, by some divine intervention, was on the scene when you so desperately needed him?"

"Too right, chief," replied Sniff, "I could-a croaked couldn't I, bloody bled to death right there on the bloody street."

"Bloodied street indeed," hammed the theatrical QC as he performed his practised flouncy flop into the chair behind him.

Simon stood to address the court,

"Your honour, my learned friend and ladies and gentlemen of the jury, the defence will not at this time keep Mr Taylor in the witness box any longer. It is clear the efforts of giving evidence have tired him. However, we will be recalling him, if we may, as part of the defence when my learned friend has concluded."

Had he looked back at Jo, he would have seen her pale face and the harrowed look of worry. She had known, of course, what Simon's strategy would be, but she hadn't been prepared for the power of Taylor's evidence. Her mind was saying that Simon should attack him now, while his evidence was fresh in the jury members' minds, but she had to be guided by him and trust him too. It was not easy for her.

From the visitor's gallery, Dan had a more remote view of proceedings and had watched the varying reactions of everyone on the jury as the prosecution case progressed. He, too, was surprised by the accusations and descriptions Taylor poured out, but he could see that the jury, initially shocked that Taylor seemed to be slightly intoxicated, had not warmed to him during his evidence. For the first time in a long time, he felt hope.

For Peter Philips, the home straight was in sight. All he had to do was discredit Jo Hadge and diminish her defence to the extent that the jury would believe she had, in fact, aimed a potentially deadly stabbing at a benevolent would-be helper. He knew, just as Dan did, that the jury had been affected by Taylor's dissolute manner, but he had to hope that the strength of his evidence had overcome any early prejudice. He knew, too, that the defendant created a demure and modestly attractive presence; she portrayed innocence and self-containment, and she had a demeanour he had to subvert.

Philips stood up again, straightened his back and focussed his gimlet eye on the jury members in turn.

"Your honour, ladies and gentlemen of the jury, I now call the defendant, Joanne Hadge, to the witness box."

She knew it was coming. She knew she had to face it. She had worried about it, planned for it, rehearsed it and played through how it might run time and time again in her mind. Compose yourself, girl, she thought, as she was released from the dock by the court usher and escorted to the witness box.

Jo took the oath and made all the preliminary detail confirmations.

Philips, too, had planned for this. To achieve the decision with which his CPS masters had tasked him, he knew that a softly-softly approach wouldn't work. He'd decided to go in hard, shake her and break her, use his skills to elicit incriminating answers from this vulnerable girl.

"Ms Hadge," he barked. "You are accused of causing grievous bodily harm with intent, that is to say, you deliberately launched a potentially lethal attack on a man who was trying to help you; you unleashed an aimed, premeditated stabbing strike, followed by a vicious physical assault with one intention, the intention of causing as much injury to a man who had done you no harm whatsoever, a man who was trying to be your knight in shining armour, your saviour bravely coming to your aid without knowing what danger he might face, not knowing that the danger would come from you, his friend who he was attempting to protect…"

"Questions, not statement Mr Philips," the judge interjected.

Philips nodded in acquiescence and returned his glare to Jo.

"Ms Hadge, what did you think when you heard knocking on your front door?"

Jo felt the calm that comes when anticipation gives way to actuality. She breathed in slowly, looked at the jury and then back at the prosecutor.

"Can we start, sir, by dealing in fact for a change? Any knocking on my door was subsequent to my doorbell being rung. The doorbell makes a sound and emits a bright light in my kitchen, and because it was being rung in a sustained way, I had to get out of bed and rush to the kitchen to switch it off, to stop it from keeping on ringing. It was when I switched the bell off that I heard banging and knocking on the door."

"If you say so, but you still haven't answered my question, Ms Hadge, I asked you what you thought when you heard someone at your door?"

"I was asleep. You know how it is when you are woken up suddenly? I didn't know what was happening; all I could hear was my doorbell, and all I could see was the doorbell alarm unit light flashing from my kitchen. I didn't know what to think except it was all so, you know, insistent, that I thought someone must be in trouble."

"I see. Were you frightened at all, Ms Hadge?

"Well, no, not really, I didn't have time to think about anything else but shutting the bell up and wondering what on earth was going on."

"So not frightened then?"

"No."

"But you still went to answer the door without knowing who it was or why they were knocking on your door in the early hours?"

"Yes, I was worried that someone may be hurt or injured or ill or needing help, so of course, I went to open the door."

"Why didn't you call the police? Most young women on their own being awoken so suddenly by someone banging on their door at night would immediately call the police. Why didn't you?"

"I just didn't even think of it. Perhaps, in hindsight, it would have been a good idea, but it just didn't cross my mind at the time. As I said, I was feeling confused and alarmed, but my first thought was that someone might need help, not that I might be about to be attacked on my doorstep."

"Let me be clear. You didn't feel fear, and you say you didn't know who was at the door or why," Peter paused for effect and cast a knowing glance at the jury, "you didn't know what was happening, you didn't think of calling the police for protection, you didn't feel fear but you selected, yes that has to be right, you deliberately selected the sharpest, longest knife you have, at least I assume you don't have anything more lethal in your kitchen than a carving knife, and armed yourself with it with the only possible intent of causing injury to whoever was at your door?"

"No, that's just not how it was. The knife was just the nearest utensil to hand on my draining board, and although I didn't feel frightened, I didn't know what was happening and I did, instinctively, feel I might need to protect myself which of course was right, I did need to protect myself."

"As with your earlier comment about facts, Ms Hadge, what is true and what is a fabrication, what caused your violent attack and why you chose to arm yourself so lethally is a matter for the jury to decide, not for you to tell us."

Jo stepped back from the front of the witness box as if recoiling from a slap. It was an involuntary action, but it was noticed, with some sympathy, by the jury. The prosecutor noticed too but going even more on the offensive was his only tactic now. He pressed on,

"Let us continue, Ms Hadge, to the circumstances of your attack."

"It was me being attacked!"

"Please limit yourself to answering my questions, Ms Hadge. We will get to the real truth, not your version of it, quicker that way. To continue, yes, to the circumstances of your attack. You went to your front door and looked through the spyhole, didn't you and so you saw the victim, who you knew very well, and that's when you decided to attack him, correct Ms Hadge?"

Simon had half-stood in an expression of objection and, his point made to the jury, sat again.

"That's not right at all, that's just not correct," she emphasised in mockery of the prosecutor's word. "I did look through the spy hole and I did see a man who I later recognised as Taylor, he was swaying and slightly bent over as if in great pain, that's why I opened the door."

"Ms Hadge, you are telling the court that on your doorstep that night was a man you recognised, who you thought was in pain but, even so, you deliberately and violently attacked him with a knife. Is that really what you want to say to the jury?"

"That's just rubbish. When I opened the door and saw it was Taylor, I could see instantly that, as usual, he was drunk or stoned or both and that he wasn't hurt or injured, he just wanted to force his way into my property. I opened the door slightly, and he yelled something at me about being, and I'm afraid this is what he said, a fucking cow and bitch. He pushed against the door ramming his foot in the doorway. I tried to slam the door closed, but his foot stopped me, and his body weight forced it further open. That's when I was terrified, that's when I knew I'd have to defend myself. That's what happened, that's how it was."

"Your front door has a safety chain, doesn't it, Ms Hadge? Why didn't you keep the chain on? Was it because you knew who was on your doorstep, and you wanted to attack him?"

"Yes, there is a chain on the door, but I released it as soon as I saw what I thought was Taylor looking to be in pain. I just didn't think to leave it hooked up when I opened the door as I didn't know then that he wasn't in pain, just drunk. It is rubbish to suggest I attacked the man. He was out of his head like normal, everyone knows he's a druggie with form for violence, a police record, and he was attacking me; I don't understand why you are protecting him."

It was like the detonation of a neutron bomb as an invisible shockwave pulsed through the courtroom. Judge Jennifer Gordon reacted instantly.

"Ladies and gentlemen," her eyes gleamed with urgency as she spoke hurriedly to the jury, "you must disregard what you have just heard from the defendant. I shall have to ask you all to leave the court while I confer with both counsellors to determine whether these proceedings will now be a mistrial or not."

The jury filed out, looking bemused. When the court had cleared, the Judge called both barristers forward.

"Mr Farrow," she glared aggressively at the defence lawyer, "your client has just broken one of the most crucial laws of evidence as well you know, and as her barrister, such an egregious breach is your responsibility. The defendant has just told the jury that the witness and putative victim has a criminal record and I can't allow that in my court."

Simon gathered his thoughts. The innocence and freedom of his client depended on his mental agility and legal ingenuity in the next few minutes.

19

Spray saw his regular hire chauffeur waiting for him at the Arrivals gate at Terminal Seven of New York's JFK airport.

Yadiel Alvarado grinned at his familiar customer and took over steering the luggage trolley.

"Hola, Signor Spray, you have a good flight? Looking good for a gringo!"

"Yadiel," responded Spray, giving his driver a friendly man-hug, "less of the gringo, more of the Sir if you don't mind!"

"Si, Siiir, ciertamente siiir."

They made their way through the terminal, past Balducci's, through the crowds of travellers, some looking lost, some looking cross, some looking excited, and some just travel weary. They walked out into the sunshine and to the nearly new five-litre supercharged Jaguar XJ with which Yadiel made part of his living. Spray settled into the soft black leather opulence of the car's rear seat as it purred and growled, as a Jaguar should, swiftly and smoothly along the Van Wyck Expressway from the airport.

"How's it been going while I've been away?"

"Good, Signor Spray, very good, the jefes are all very happy with us still, so I am very happy, and you'll be very happy too, business is good, very good signor."

Spray looked out of his window as Van Wyck became Grand Central Highway. The Jaguar swept past Corona Park, and his mind started to meander; how had he got into all this, and where would it all lead?

It had all begun, he mused, with Jimmy Lopez, a clever and engaging fellow cybersecurity grad at MIT who had shown Spray a different world. Jimmy drove a replica Bullitt Mustang, once owned by a rock star. He ate at Rare in Encore Boston Harbour hotel complex and gambled in its famous and exclusive casino. Jimmy had money, and he knew how to spend it.

"Do you gamble a lot?" Spray had asked him.

"I don't have to pay for my dinner," replied Lopez.

Spray and Jimmy became good friends as they studied together. They pushed each other intellectually and technically. Spray loved the good life that Jimmy shared with him, and Jimmy valued the motivation and alternative, often insightful, views that Spray provided. It was an easy-going relationship; neither asked questions about the other, neither judged nor criticised. They simply got on, enjoying their learning as much as they enjoyed a vigorous social life, sharing laughter, pranks and girlfriends in youthful trust and mutual happiness.

When Spray told Jimmy about his love of powerboat racing, Jimmy imported an Italian-designed DAC F1 powerboat from the UK.

"My family loves all sports," Jimmy assured Spray, "and I'll get some sponsorship money from them, don't worry, we'll have a season of fun, and then, probably, we sell it again, and everyone's happy!"

For a year anyway, Spray could shun the memory of being Spray the football tack man and become Spray the powerboat racer, and he was very close to being in heaven. It was all true; racers did have a great life of high-speed sport punctuated by irresponsible antics, boozy parties and a non-stop supply of girls.

The perfectionist in Spray, the quality which would make him successful in any endeavour, drove him to be as fit as he could be, trim, slim and honed to be race-ready. Spray was pleased with himself in his white, green and red overalls and helmet and matching tricolour hull.

"Don't look in the water and see your reflection," one of his girlfriends had teased, "it didn't do Narcissus any good."

Jimmy and Spray travelled together but were often joined at

race meetings by groups of Jimmy's family who usually flew up from Mexico in their modified long-distance Cessna Caravan aeroplane. Jimmy's dark-eyed, dark-haired cousin Margarita usually shepherded the groups. She led her party of relatives around the powerboat pits to where the family's party gazebo would be erected; it was also white, green and red and gave Spray's team an air of cosmopolitan sophistication.

"It may be Mentor, Ohio," Spray told himself, "but it could be Monaco." It was only in later years, after a lot of travelling, that Spray realised he'd rather be in Mentor, Ohio than Monaco anyway.

"Why do we have everything in Italian colours?" asked Spray of his chum.

"It's not Italian, you dummy," responded his friend called Lopez, "it's obviously as Mexican as I am; you should take up vexillology, and then you'd know your flag colours. And, you know what, I think it looks cool as a racing livery, and it makes us easy to find at any event, which is also pretty cool."

"Why do we need to be easy to find Jimmy? It's only your family who come to our races, and they always know where we'll be."

"Yeah, but they, you know, like to invite a few folks along for the gig, just to be sociable and telling guests to look out for our colours makes it easy, eh?"

Spray had noticed a steady stream of guests coming to the gazebo for drinks and nibbles, all organised by the excellent Margarita. She had a seemingly endless supply of white, green and red racing livery goody bags for the visitors, many of whom appeared to be more interested in their bags than the racing. Spray's infatuation with Margarita grew every time he saw her and, as the season progressed, he felt an exciting affinity and affection for her. Overtly flirty, Margarita teased Spray constantly; he felt close to her one moment and a million miles away the next.

It was at one of the last races of the season, away from Spray's favoured Ohio venues, at romantic Key West, Florida, that Margarita, fixing Spray with a seductive gaze, walked to him slowly and rattled his world with a long, full-on, passionate kiss. Feeling like a schoolboy, Spray trembled, stuttered and felt his face warming as Margarita leant slightly away from him and giggled knowingly. Spray was relieved to be wearing his restrictive fireproof suit, or his outstanding embarrassment would have been complete.

Spray's black hair, blue eyes, and slightly battered features often appealed to girls. He was used to flattering attention, but Margarita was different; she made him want to prove himself, show his manliness, and he had to admit to himself, do anything to please her.

"C'mon Spray darling," she murmured as she put her arm under his and pulled him towards her, "let's pose for the cameraman."

And there he was, a man from somewhere behind the team gazebo, firing off shots on his electro-optical Canon. Spray and Margarita moved from pose to pose, holding hands, in an embrace and with Margarita and Spray holding a team goody-bag in a presentation stance.

"What's in all these bags anyway?" asked Spray again, for possibly the hundredth time.

"Just photos of you and the boat, some mini Zeiss binoculars, some luxury chocs, a commemorative programme; just the usual stuff, nothing you'd be interested in, honey,"

Spray was far too distracted to question any further.

After many more races and moments with Margarita, the season ended with Spray having scored some reasonable successes. As he had said, Jimmy arranged for the boat to be sold, and the two friends turned their minds back to their studies, which were also about to reach their end.

The exhilaration of racing and the excitement of MIT soon

began to fade, and, for a while, Jimmy and Spray went off to create the rest of their lives, Jimmy back to Mexico and one of the family firms and Spray to DueDilig in London.

Spray spent as much time as he could on video calls with Margarita, who continued to tantalise him, and with Jimmy, with whom he shared his new experiences and developed his new dreams.

"I'm going to come back to the States soon," Spray announced in a video call with Jimmy and Margarita. "It's been two years here and I've learned as much as I think I can. So, I guess it's crunch time, I gotta find me some money, some serious, professional backing and I'm starting my own outfit."

The three chatted over the link for some time as Spray outlined his plans for what would be Onetelcall and why he'd kick off in Ohio with, he believed, a couple of clients already in the pipeline.

Jimmy met Spray at Cleveland Hopkins airport. Spray had slept for the first leg of his trip from Heathrow to Atlanta, where the flight stopped over for three hours, but felt restless and agitated for the two or so hours on to Ohio. His mind relished the challenge of building a business and making a great life for himself but the bird of practicality sitting on his shoulder squawked words of warning about start-up and working capital and paying for the advanced and costly tech development he had designed and specified.

"You look cansado, plain dead tired, my old friend, bad flight?"

"No, Jimmy, it was a fine flight and it's great to be home. London was an unforgettable and great experience, and I loved every second, but here is where I want to be and here is where I want to start up my giant global corporation, if I can find the bucks I need to fire it all up, that's probably why I look so beat."

"Then listen up, amigo, I may have words to smooth out the lines on your worried brow," Jimmy was grinning so happily,

Spray wondered if he'd been drinking. "I have described your vision to some of my family and I've told them what a genius and all-round good fella you are, and guess what, go on, guess what."

"I can't, Jimmy, I can't guess what, but I can see you are bursting to tell me what, so why don't you do just that?"

"It's this, Spray, you see, my family is quite rich, and they make their money in many ways, a sort of conglomeration of interests. They think they'd like to provide you with the dollars you need to set up and get all your R&D and production going. All you gotta do is provide a spreadsheet and some bottom-line numbers, and that's it, abracadabra, you're in business and ready to rule the world."

"Oh Jimmy, that's fantastic, just fantastic," Spray's mind was in hyperdrive as he assimilated what he'd just heard, but his pragmatic nature soon kicked in. "It can't be just as easy as that, can it, Jimmy? I mean, what about repayment, what about security for the loan if it is a loan or shares, you know, a bit of the action as they say, or someone telling me what to do or someone I have to report to, see what I mean? Don't think I'm not massively grateful, 'cos I am, you know I am, but I have to ask what the terms are, what's the quid pro quo, what would I be signing up for?"

"Hey, guy, don't fret. It's cool, it is, I wouldn't give you a deal that ties you up, nor would my family; we're honourable people, you know," Jimmy emphasised 'honourable' in a way Spray found a little intimidating, but he glossed over it.

"You have the money you need, and we don't ask for anything from you except that you make a success of it and when, and for sure you will, you wanna go for a float on Nasdaq, they will expect a bunch of preferential shares which is only fair I'd say, but the lawyers will write it all up for you to read, understand and sign, Ok?"

"Yeah, Jimmy, yeah, that's beyond awesome. I don't know what to say to you and all your family. I mean, they can have as many shares as they want by then 'cos I'll have made it big time.

We must all get together so I can thank them, what do you say?"

"Relax, bud, no need for a big gratitude production. We don't go in for all, that, we like to prove our thanks by deed and action, know what I mean? All our businesses work together, so there'll be times when one of the other enterprises needs something you can provide, and with everything you've learned since our time at MIT, they'll value your expertise. Sometimes, it may be something that has nothing to do with security, or it might just be delivering legal papers or other stuff if you're travelling somewhere where we have interests, that sort of thing. Anyway, don't worry about it because I expect any little bits of inter-company activity will come through me anyway so it will be cool."

"Well," said Spray, wondering what other little favours he'd be asked to provide, "I'll for sure be travelling a great deal, so if you need a safe pair of hands to courier contracts and the like, then I'm your man." As he was speaking, Spray began to wonder what else Jimmy's 'family' might be involved in and from nowhere, a shiver ran down his spine.

Prescience can be a worrying trait, he thought, as Jimmy gripped his arm and said,

"Y'gotta look in your eyes, compadre, that I can read real easy, seen it before so many times y'see. You're wondering just what you're getting into, and you're getting suspicions, man, you're getting dark vibes 'cos nothing that looks this good can come without a catch, risk or some danger, am I right or am I right?"

"You're right, Jimmy, and I'm sorry to have doubts about you and what you and your family are offering, and I'd like to believe that it is all in the name of investment and profit, of nurturing new enterprise and creating new business. Somehow, I get the feeling there's more to it than altruism or entrepreneurship. Level with me, Jimmy, we've come too far together for you not to be straight."

"Ok, bud. Here's the thing. You know me as well as anyone

can, and you know I got loyalty. I got loyalty to my family, and that always comes first, then I got loyalty to my friends, and you, Spray, are my best friend so you got my best-friend loyalty. We call it lealtad, bud, lealtad. It's what keeps us alive, and it can be what kills us."

Spray nodded in understanding, now knowing what was about to come.

"So, get to the business end, Jimmy, tell me about the business, tell me about what can get us killed, Jimmy, tell me about the drugs."

"Then I don't need to Spray, you are already there. I can give you all the background, tell you about Mexico and its cartels, tell you about our supplies from Argentina, Peru, Bolivia, Ecuador and Colombia; hell, we've even got our own farms in the south of Mexico. I can tell you about it all, but what's to know? I can tell you about our routes under the airport into Texas, our distribution around the US and how we've extended our network at each and every powerboat meeting you've raced at; remember the gift bags?"

Spray did, indeed, remember the gift bags, the photos, the explanations from Margarita, and he knew he was in it up to his neck already. In that moment of realisation, Spray felt a seismic shift in his mind; it was a Solzhenitsyn moment when the battle line between good over evil ran through his heart, or was it greed over sense? Either way, Spray's conscience offered no defence. He would deal in death, but he would have his business and be wealthy, powerful, and successful. Part of him knew it was always going to be this way.

"Jimmy, when I was a tack-spray boy in pro sport, I saw ruthless, I saw lives made and lives broken, I saw people keep their principles and lose their chance of fortunes, and I saw exactly what can be achieved with cold-blooded determination. From how we went racing, you know that feelings for my fellow man aren't high in my priorities. From all that we've done together, you knew that we'd be having a conversation like this and, for sure, I believe I knew it too. You and your family, you've got a deal, Jimmy and I'll move heaven and earth to make sure it's a great deal for all of us." Spray held out his hand, and his future path was determined.

Now, in the back of Yadiel Alvarado's Jag, those memories and that handshake seemed like several lifetimes ago, remembered in the twenty minutes it took to travel from JFK to La Guardia, where Spray's company seaplane was hangared close to the old Pan Am Clipper building.

Spray said thanks and goodbye to Yadiel and prepared himself for two hours of joy, piloting his modified Cessna 182 floatplane back to Ohio and his private waterside air deck on a hidden lake just off Interstate 90.

20

Simon was prepared. In his many conversations with Jo, he had been struck by her outrage that the authorities had done so little to curb Sniff Taylor's well-known activities.

"Everyone knows, the whole town knows what a shit he is," Jo had declared more than a few times. "He got one of his own gang sent to prison, he peddles dope all over the place, he's violent and evil, and yet the police do nothing. Why? I ask you. Why? What's he got that's keeping him so safe from the law? It's outrageous, and I shall say so to anyone who'll listen."

"Not in court, Jo," the barrister had explained, "the laws about disclosure of previous crimes are very strict, and if you sound off about Sniff's past malfeasance, you'll be held in contempt and the trial will be stopped without hesitation. The judge would rule a mistrial and that would be very bad for us, for your defence."

Jo had nodded in reluctant acquiescence but, if she'd thought about so doing, she'd have had her fingers crossed. Now, Simon's worst expectations had become reality, and he was faced with an irate judge and a raptor-like prosecuting adversary. Some might have felt intimidated, but not Simon, his tremulous days were long behind him.

Armed with research and precedents and every interpretation of the criminal procedures acts, plus the CPS's very own policies and Disclosure: A Protocol for the Control and Management of Unused Material in the Crown Court, Simon set about winning Judge Jennifer over with his unique mix of logic and law.

Jennifer Gordon had no bias, no prejudice, no 'isms or 'phobics, especially when sitting in judgement. Privately, she may harbour a view or two about unfairness, unearned entitlement and the vicious, cowardly mendacity of anonymous social media trolls, but she'd never air them beyond a protected environment.

Drugs, more the selling than the buying, were her pet bete noire, and she was struggling to keep her powerful antipathy to pushers under control in the case of the repellent Kevin Taylor.

Fortunately for her, Simon had done his job well. He proffered arguments so strong about his client's disclosure and the continuance of the trial that even the often-captious Philip Peters had to accede. Jennifer declared, after appropriate admonishment, the trial's recommencement.

"Ladies and gentlemen," Judge Jennifer addressed the returned jury, "you will have gathered that any disclosures of any witness's previous life are not a matter for this court. Such a comment is to be ignored totally as it may not even be valid, and you will certainly not be able to assess its worth or veracity. Strike from your memories, please, that last outburst from the defendant and give it no place in your considerations. Your job and your only job is to listen to all the evidence, consider that evidence carefully and responsibly and conclude, unanimously if possible, whether there is guilt or whether there is no guilt according to the charges brought. I will give you guidance at the end of the evidence. I will also give you my comments and summation, but it will be you, collectively, who will decide in this matter, without any need for any extraneous admissions to be included in your deliberations. I hope that is clear."

The jurors, comically thought Dan, nodded in unison. The nodding then changed from up and down to more tennis-match style side-to-side as the questioning tussle between Peters and Hadge resumed.

"Ah, Ms Hadge, now that we have all seen an example of your uncontrolled temper and ill-advised actions."

"Mr Peters…" warned the judge.

"Quite so," replied the prosecutor to the unsaid rebuke. "Ms Hadge, do you feel you can carry on and give honest and factual answers to my questions?"

Jo seethed inside but disciplined herself to appear calm and assured.

Philip Peters also seethed. Although he was adopting his best ferocious look and his in-for-the-kill forward-leaning stance, he was quietly cursing his paymasters in the CPS. It was no surprise to him that the CPS attracted such public and professional criticism.

A succession of DPPs had whitewashed over the apparent deficiencies of the organisation for years. It was accused, often with some justification, of dropping challenging, difficult cases and of openly, and in some instances, erroneously and harmfully, pursuing celebrity cases at the cost of more serious crime prosecutions, of collaborating with the media and relying too much on police influence. The CPS was, in Philip Peters' view, responsible for the tsunami of serious common crime. Like many public bodies, he would argue, the CPS was overweight in administration and middle management, frittered money needlessly on non-productive expenditure, was unsympathetic to victims, and inefficient in prosecution case preparation.

In the matter of Regina versus Hadge, he knew that an inexperienced paralegal had managed the file, had insisted that the charge be the more consequential 'with intent' without the necessary compelling evidence, and tasked him with securing a conviction without equipping him with the required weapons.

Jo's aberration – or was it quite deliberate? – had offered him a slim chance of showing her to have an unbridled temper and capable of extreme spontaneous violence. However, his courtroom sensitivity told him that the judge wouldn't tolerate such a spin, and the jury would probably veer towards sympathising with Jo rather than condemning her. But Philip Peters didn't give up that easily.

"Before your outburst, we had established some basic facts, these being that you woke up to a ringing doorbell, that you picked up a sharp knife, that you claim you didn't see Mr Taylor through your front door spy hole but opened the door anyway and that you then plunged your knife into Mr Taylor's neck narrowly avoiding murdering him on your doorstep; these are the facts aren't they, Ms Hadge?"

Again, Simon stood to intervene, but Judge Jennifer Gordon favoured him with a glance that said, 'leave it' and then she looked at Jo in the witness box with an expectant expression.

Jo's fury had abated, replaced with the confidence and logic of justification and honesty. She knew that any court hearing had an element of 'the show' about it, that the jury was an audience, and that guile would be more effective than verbal conflict.

"Your honour, Mr Peters, I have already said exactly what happened, how I felt, how and why I reacted as I did to the most terrifying of circumstances. I will not give credibility to the prosecution's version of events; I will not argue the position because I was there, Mr Taylor was there, but no one else was there. Any interpretations of what happened are just that, speculative and without any merit. Either I'm telling the truth, or I am not. Going over it time and time again until Mr Peters gets an answer which suits him is not a game I'm going to play. Your honour, I will, of course, answer any and all direct questions, but I don't think it is right to expect me to play verbal ping-pong with the prosecution unless you direct me so to do."

Simon smiled inwardly. That's a girl with some guts, he thought, with a sense of pride that surprised him.

Judge Jennifer, who had expected some feistiness, also had to hide her admiration.

"Ms Hadge, the court thanks you for your direct comments. However, you cannot decide what you will or won't say. This court is here to establish facts, nothing else. Mr Peters will ask questions, and you will answer. Mr Peters will, I am sure, refrain from postulation and theorising. Let us now continue, please, Mr Peters."

Bugger that thought Peters, knowing he was on the back foot again. He knew he'd get nowhere with further questioning and, risking another Judge Jennifer ticking-off, he went for a preclosing speech lunge.

"Thank you, your honour, indeed no more postulation because none is necessary. The facts as I have described them are not theory, they are the actuality. I have no more questions for Ms Hadge, no more witnesses because the Crown has established its case for all reasonable, intelligent people to see and understand, as my closing comments will confirm."

Simon, relieved that the hearing had come so far without any significant prosecution body-blows, decided on a riskier, high-impact strategy.

"Your honour, and you, the jury," he looked at each of the jurors quickly in turn with a benign, engaging eye, "it is my belief too that we have all heard the evidence we need. We have heard from specialist witnesses who disbelieved any 'intent' accusation. We have heard evidence of a relationship between my client and the witness Mr Taylor but established only the unlikelihood of this. We have heard, more or less," Simon showed an ironic smile, "from Mr Taylor who was indeed verbose, even garrulous but whose evidence, I suggest, is questionable and whose state of mind during this trial surely raises questions in your minds about his veracity and plausibility.

"And we have heard from my client, Jo Hadge, and I feel that we can all relate to her testimony. So, before you warn me, your honour, for making a speech, may I say that I would like to offer the jury some real, incontrovertible, tangible evidence of the events of that terrible night. I would like to show a video CD, supplied as evidence by the CPS itself. It is a view of Ms Hadge's very front door from a security camera belonging to the public house 'The Coopers.' With your permission, your honour, I will show this now."

A large screen monitor was placed in front of the jury, and the courtroom lights were dimmed. The video played. A dark, grainy image showed Sniff walking unsteadily backwards and forwards past the flat's street entry door. It showed him standing in the doorway as the door was opened. It showed him moving forwards and then staggering backwards as an arm could be seen to be coming down towards him from inside the doorway. It showed the entire occurrence.

The jury was captivated and asked to see it several times, studying it carefully and attentively frame by frame until they declared they had seen enough.

Jo from the dock and Dan from the visitor's gallery watched the jury's reaction with grim fascination. Did the CD prove anything? One way or another? Were they swayed, convinced, or dubious?

Inexorably, the hearing was reaching its climax. The judge's summation and guiding comments to the jury would follow closing comments from the defender and prosecutor. Jo's mind, previously agile and urgent, had slipped into a pressure-induced torpor, its acuity dulled to lethargy. She listened to the final proceedings but absorbed only the more strident elements. She gazed at the jury, wondering if they were about to levy an inconceivable penalty of guilt and imprisonment.

Dan was cramped with anxiety. His body felt taut and rigid, mouth dry, mind numb, his distressed eyes scanning the courtroom as he tried to find sense, any sense, out of the whole catastrophe. A torrent of abstract thoughts attacked his subconsciousness. He'd marry her in prison, he'd exact great revenge on the vile Sniff, he'd mount a one-man crusade against violence and drug dealing, and he'd love her forever. Oh God, let us have a life after this torture. A hand seized his shoulder; fingers dug into him. He turned, surprised to see a white-faced, tense Max Golby behind. Dan tried to smile his heartfelt appreciation, and Max grinned weakly in support and comradeship.

The prosecution's closing comments were predictably forceful and colourful. Hadn't the jury seen for themselves the defendant's lack of control, her fractious temper, her headstrong reactions? Of course, she saw Taylor through the spyhole. Of course, he knew her, and she knew him. He needed her help and she, furious and malicious, had knowingly and deliberately stabbed him, aimed at his most vulnerable spot. Why would she have a knife otherwise? Why else didn't she call the police?

She had lied and lied again, believing, with all the vanity of the spoiled and indulged woman she is, that you, the jury, would be gullible, easily won over and believe her more than the older, less attractive, less clever and quite bewildered victim who can't understand why his attacker is making him out to be the villain. Oh yes, she knew it was him at the door, and she selected her sharpest knife to inflict the most harm she could. There can be no doubt, and careful observation of the video shows her terrible, callous act in grim reality. You can see her arm swinging, her carefully-selected, long, sharp, deadly knife plunging into the innocent, hurt victim who had to stagger away from her vicious, murderous attack to find lifesaving help elsewhere.

Now, the jury looked pensive. The prosecution conspectus had found its mark, and the jurors' faces showed it. Dan, with Max's hand still on his shoulder, could see it. Max could see it. Jo, unsure of what was happening now felt a sudden unease and, most of all, Simon could see it.

Jo heard Simon start to talk, his voice soft and authoritative. No bluster, no bravado. Calm and gentle. That must be good, she thought. She heard him confirm the expert witness's view that denied culpable intent. She heard a firm repudiation of any over-familiarity between her and Taylor; she heard Simon quietly and without any rancour, diminish the evidence given by Taylor. She was relieved to hear Simon's rational and plausible description of precisely what happened and, even in her current disassociated state, knew he was leading the jury to the video, the, hopefully, damning film noir.

Judge Jennifer Gordon felt a sense of relief too. It had been a difficult trial for her as she couldn't help but feel sympathy for Jo and repugnance for Kevin Taylor. Being a judge places a great strain on one's impartiality, she thought. She summed up with equitable objectivity. She reviewed what was fact and what was opinion and cited potential errors of evidence and areas of doubt.

She highlighted the certainties and emphasised the responsibility of the jury, and the effect a wrong decision might have on at least two lives. She explained, with feeling, how a juror's reaction, view and judgement of a witness, or indeed an accused, good or bad, had to be forsaken in the pursuit of honesty and justice. She guided them in matters of law and referred to the immutable credibility of the video evidence submitted by the CPS. She dispatched the jury for its deliberations and, preferably, a unanimous decision.

The jury was syphoned off to the appropriate room, complete with hot and cold drinks and, of course, biscuits. Philip Peters, looking fussed and florid, ran for the cover of the rooms set aside for the CPS. He was downcast to see Taylor and some flabby chap lolling arrogantly against his favourite chair.

Dan and Max left the visitors' seats and met Simon and Jo in the hall area. Dan and Jo clung to one another for a long time, longer than may be considered seemly, while a slightly embarrassed Max introduced himself to the still be-wigged and robed Simon.

There was a vending machine-cum-café area next to what passed as the barristers' robing room. As a café, it had nothing to recommend it, scruffy, uncomfortable and somehow hostile, but it was, at least, somewhere for them all to sit and drink some much-needed caffeine.

The conversation was nervous, jerky, and stilted.

"Max, I don't know how to thank you for coming here today, I really appreciate it. All Ok at base, I take it?"

"No probs boss," replied a tense Max, knowing that the only issue on everyone's mind was the verdict.

"Oh Dan," murmured Jo. "Dan, I just can't stand this; it's terrible, isn't it? What a complete load of shit. Oh, Simon, how can I thank you? No matter what the result is, I couldn't have asked for more than you did today; you're a clever man, and I'm glad you're on my side."

Simon was unusually touched. "Jo, I have to say I feel a tiny bit confident; you know I have faith in our British justice system, and we were lucky with the judge we got and, I think, with the jury selection. But, even so, we can never be sure, but I'm with you whatever happens."

Then a contemplative silence took over. A sip, a grimace, more coffee, nothing to eat, no one could eat.

"Simon," ventured Max, "how long does this sort of thing usually take? I mean, how long will the jury take to make its mind up do you think?"

Simon looked at Max, understanding that his question had been asked for everyone's benefit. "Lap of the gods' old chap, lap of the gods' with the added length of a piece of string."

As if predetermined by the gods of tension, the internal PA system hissed, "Case of Hadge, case of Hadge, return to court."

Jo felt as if she were about to combust spontaneously, so great was the pressure on her. Was this it? The verdict?

But no, the court reassembled and the jury's chairperson, a tall, middle-aged man in an expensive suit, stood to say,

"We would like to ask, please, if we may see the videotape again?"

They watched the difficult sequence several times. They took it in turns to move closer to the screen and peer at the low-quality movie images. The jurors made entre-nous comments to each other and squinted again at another replay. Then they headed back to their den of decision.

Twice they did this. Twice they returned to the courtroom for more video analysis. Twice more, Jo thought her fate was about to be announced. She was close to collapse, close to tears, close to hysterics. How could anyone bear this cruel suspense?

Simon feared that the jury might hang it out and claim their night, dinner and drinks included, at one of Reading's better hotels. Some of the jurors looked to him as though they'd grasp a freebie if they could. The chairperson, though, in the good suit, didn't look like he'd want a night in a Reading hotel, free or not, and he pinned his hopes on him being the driving force.

Evidently, the chair carried the day; no night away from home for him. The court reconvened by mid-afternoon. Everyone took their place and waited in silence. Dan saw. with some disgust, Sniff Taylor and his mate take a seat in the visitors' gallery, but as far away from him and Max as possible.

Each minute, which felt like ten minutes, increased the tension until, at last, the knock was heard, and Judge Jennifer Gordon took her imposing seat for the last time in this case.

Everyone knew the words before they were spoken,

"Have you reached a conclusion, are you all agreed?"

The good suit stood, answer ready on his lips as he looked first at the visitors' gallery and involuntarily raised his eyebrows when he saw Sniff, and next, he looked at Dan and Max. Then his eyes went to the two barristers and finally settled on what he thought to be the delightful sight of the judge.

She asked. He answered.

"Not guilty."

Just two words, they take next to no time to say but an age to comprehend. Jo didn't move for a full five seconds and then sat back down, head in hands and tears creating streaked black patterns on her cheeks. Dan thought Max's hand was going to extract his clavicle from its mountings; both of them were sighing and still shaking slightly.

Judge Jennifer Gordon stood; the court stood. And then it was empty. It was over. Except for Sniff and Lardy, who remained seated in the visitors' gallery, Sniff's face twisted and contorted with mindless fury.

21

There had been background stories running in the press and on social media for some time, but no one had taken much notice. There was a new illness spreading virulently in China's Hubei province, and because news coming from the province was scarce and sparse, the rest of the world didn't feel spurred into any active precaution. More news eventually seeped from the Peoples' Republic as Hubei's major city, Wuhan, reported an epidemic scale of deaths from what they had identified as a pneumonia-like novel coronavirus SARS-CoV-2. By December, the world had become aware that it faced a horrendous pandemic.

The Huanan live animal and seafood market in Wuhan was claimed to be the origination of the virus at the time, although Chinese scientists and some experts from the World Health Organisation disputed this. They also denied accusations that the virus emanated from Wuhan's Institute of Virology, whether by accident or design.

Covid-19 hit an unwarned, unprepared world with demonic ferocity. Millions of people died. Governments around the world and of all hues were plunged into panic. Unsure and inexperienced, they looked at the science, they feared daily mass deaths. They shored up ailing health services, pressed the 'urgent' button in their civil services, and were met with brave and selfless activity on the frontline of care and institutionalised inefficiency in some of the bureaucratic layers of management. The citizens of afflicted countries reacted with heart-warming kindness and fortitude in close communities struggling to maintain a sense of life. Around the world, there were social-media-driven shouts of 'hoax,' 'conspiracy,' and 'government control.'

As governments adopted, to various extents, a lockdown programme of limited travel and human contact, the pandemic became a little more manageable and understood. There was global competition for an antidote, a vaccination that would save the world. Arguments, objections and theories spewed from a growing anti-vax movement, even as more and more people died. Rational people became facile. Blame without alternative solutions became unusually acceptable and reaction to any restrictive dictum veered from understanding adherence to school-like disobedience.

The restriction of 'lockdown,' confining people to their homes, first met with grumbling and then with some acceptance. To unsettle communities, to undermine understanding and cooperation became a fight for disruption, a cause of which every rebel had dreamed. The unfettered channels of mass digital communication achieved world-war weapon status for the radical and subversive. Much of the world was in torment, self-destruction, and at a loss for any direction, any cogent sense of future. Countries were falling into social division even though the virus mutated, over a long time, into a less fatal foe.

The microcosm of Olderbury reflected global turmoil in its own, parochial way. Lockdown had forged friendships and forced separations. As a new day-to-day rhythm gradually evolved, businesses faced the reality of insolvency, jobs were lost, and financial and spiritual depression afflicted the town. The supermarkets boomed as panic buying came, went, came, went, came, went according to ever-changing news and social media manipulation. Home delivery driving jobs soaked up a small proportion of newly unemployed.

In the larger companies, employees stayed at home with eighty per cent of their wages being paid by the taxpayer and, for some, the lockdown wasn't too much of a hardship. For the lonely, the elderly, those in cramped houses and flats with restless, bored, frustrated children for so many people without a voice, the lockdown was almost beyond mental endurance

For some, it was too much.

Orchestrated clamouring from vociferous minorities of

various quasi-virtuous views, all shouted their angst. The mellow majority in so many countries wondered whether it would be racism, economics, civil uprising, or the marionette martyrs, the virtuous self-appointed guardians of public rectitude, who would cause the last battle of a 21st century Armageddon first.

Olderbury police were unusually joyous. They could ease up on the more challenging or threatening crimes and attend to their punctilious enforcement of a plentiful set of new rules and restrictions. Parties were gleefully sundered, streets were struttingly patrolled, visitors were sent home, and public transport was patrolled for any face mask transgressions.

The more alert and commercially aware town council members smelled an opportunity. Emergency sale freeholds from failing retail, hospitality and office businesses looked promisingly cheap, especially when any restrictions or regulations that the council could slap on a property of interest, deterred any outsiders' competitive bids.

The Covid-19 virus, for Onetelcall, meant viral growth. In the US, Spray's sales team began to believe that the Chinese president for life, Xi Jinping, was more bountiful than Santa or even the US Defence Department's technology purchasing division. There was growing global suspicion of China, its hacking capabilities, its installed 'spy' technologies, its digital disruption techniques, its commercial and territorial aspirations by stealth, and its evident ability to win wars before anyone noticed that battle had been joined.

The state's sheer scope of threat created paranoia in the sectors that Onetelcall's specialist security systems and services could address; the easiest sell the sales team had ever had.

In Dordrecht and Olderbury too, Onetelcall was reacting to a deluge of demand. Holland's mix of supermajor oil and gas giants, avionics and multi-nationals gave Max's new chum Julian Visser, Chloe's boss and Dutch country manager, his best-ever year and biggest bonus too. For Julian, Covid meant wealth.

Dan, too, was overseeing a tidal wave of expansion.

Recruiting, training, developing, promoting, and paying incentives were all rare functions in the new Coronavirus age but all very common in the frenetic activity of Onetelcall.

If Onetelcall was on a Covid-driven roll, Spray's activities with Jimmy and his family were even more frenetic as global demand for drugs surged as fast as the virus spread. Spray reflected on the irony; as businesses became bankrupt, as millions lost their livelihoods all around the world, his two sources of income, drugs and corporate fear, flourished. Devoid of any empathy or compassion, Spray smiled to himself and planned his next tryst with his only weakness, Margarita.

When the Lopez family adopted Spray, they understood that the friendship between Spray and Jimmy wasn't a good management tool, so they appointed Margarita as line boss for their valuable recruit. In the early days, she had relished her role as a femme-fatale. Spray was infatuated, and she knew it. She controlled him like a puppeteer, and he didn't notice or care. She felt little guilt. She recognised the similarities they shared. Neither understood the softness, kindness and sympathy of ordinary people. Venal and lascivious, they both regarded making love as a means to a selfish, even when jointly experienced, climactic end.

And yet, as time progressed, Margarita found that she did have feelings after all. She anticipated seeing Spray with increasing desire and with a depth of affection as strange to her as a foreign language. As much as she understood it, she loved her papa, and she loved Jimmy. Until now, she had felt nothing but occasional contempt for anyone else, but now Spray had become the third person in the world for whom she felt something approaching passion, even love.

Of course, Margarita's feelings were not like that silly, soft, sentimental pap that Spray had described when he talked about his UK buddy Dan and his girl Jo. Ugh, she thought as Spray related the tale of Jo's attack and subsequent court-hearing, how Dan had stood by her, fought for her, protected her and loved her. Ugh, she thought again, as she heard about how Dan and Jo, after the not-guilty verdict, had recuperated from their ordeal in a remote converted cowshed halfway up a Welsh mountain. A final ugh was prompted by the news that Dan had told Spray he was going to marry Jo and had asked Spray to be his best man. Margarita's final comment was short, 'pinche estupido'.

Spray often talked about Dan, and Margarita knew that here was another weakness in Spray's carapace. In fact, the whole European operation was far too lax for Margarita's liking; she preferred a more robust management style of maximum threat. There was this guy Max too. What was the story there? Spray had taken to him and trusted him far too early, far too fast. And was local distribution through some 'cabron' called Sniff, stupid enough to get himself and his supplier in court for no good reason, really as safe and controlled as it should be? Her feelings for Spray may be getting deeper, but her opinion of his management abilities was definitely waning.

She had shared her doubts with Jimmy. To her surprise, Jimmy agreed.

"He is a genius. Onetelcall has been a success beyond our expectations; its technologies are world-class, and so are the company's customers. Spray was born to achieve, and he found his niche. It was clear to me at college that he'd make it; that's why we backed him. But I'm not so sure he runs our family business quite so brilliantly. He has been a bit lax, too trusting and too hands-off. Stuff goes through Onetelcall in the UK and Europe Ok, but his European chief, Dan, is a true friend of his and, if it comes to a showdown, Spray doesn't have it in him to let Dan take the wrap like he should. I can see the time coming when we might have to dig Spray out of the mierda; make him disappear."

Margarita's eyes pinpointed as she gasped.

"No, Margarita, I don't mean 'disappeared' in the cartel way, but something more accommodating and far away from anywhere he can be found -with or without you – that'll be your choice, your decision, but think about it now 'cos I've got a feeling of inevitability, and my feelings are usually on the money, aren't they."

22

The first lockdown in the UK took Sniff by surprise. He didn't have much appetite for news and current affairs so, when most of the working population of Olderbury was suddenly at home on furlough pay, Spray felt opportunity beckon. He called a board meeting. With Arfa, Lardy and Duggie giving Sniff as much attention as they could manage, they agreed that Snifferoo was, indeed, a good idea. Similar to a food delivery service, Snifferoo would offer a doorstep service for coke or any chemical delights they could get and sell.

Duggie was tasked with the executive role of chief supply communication officer. He had to tell Slicko-fucker Max to make sure plenty of stuff was available. Arfa and Lardy were to get some key-worker hi-viz jackets, a handful of cheap SIM-only mobile phones and a couple of mopeds for starters. Sniff would see all his outlets and get the names, addresses and phone numbers of their best clients. None were in a position to be uncooperative.

Sniff ensured the home delivery business would run efficiently and safely. He recruited teenagers, youths from his estate, to be part of his team, his family, and his friends. He'd look after them, and all they had to do was deliver door-to-door as directed by one of his 'key-worker' blokes. The phones rang, the mopeds phutted around the town; the teenagers met the mopeds and, new deliveries in hand, trotted off on their rounds. Sniff had time to think, plan and prepare.

Since the trial, Sniff had been a changed man. He frightened his blokes even more. The look of hatred hadn't faded, and Sniff now sported a permanent scowl. He'd get 'em, he'd have his revenge. He'd make those two fuckers pay. Dan and Jo? Ha. They'd suffer, they'd really fucking suffer. Not by his own hand. Sniff had a plan for this too. It had happened by accident.

"'ere Sniff," whispered Eric conspiratorially from behind his bar in The Carpenters Arms. Emboldened by a secret swig or two of bubbly with Peggy, he said, "look, don't get angry, but I know what you're doing on the knocker if you get my drift. Sometimes, your blokes get a bit chatty, if you get my drift."

Sniff got Eric's drift.

"Only me and Peg 'ad a thought, didn't we? All them fuckers on their fuckin' eighty per cent wages for doin' fuck all, eh? Gets on yer tits if you get my drift. Well, this lockdown rubbish means the fuckers aren't getting to the boozers, are they? You got the answer ain't yous. If the mountain can't come to- well, you get my drift. Only I can get some real cheap voddy. It ain't the best, I'll give you that, but it does the trick and gets yer pissed well enough. I can get lots of it for next to sweet fuck all. Knocked off yer know. Understand?"

Sniff understood.

"Well, your boys could deliver my voddy too, couldn't they? We could both make a nice few quid, eh? What ya say, Sniff? Yous ain't cross, are you? Only it's a shame to see a good thing on offer without doin' it, if you get...."

Sniff held up his hand. He couldn't stand any more drifting.

"Eric, Eric, Eric. You and Peggy sure you want to get into all this? The local plod may be as thick as, but if you're caught, you might get banged up. It's risky, Eric, well risky."

"I know, Sniff. I wouldn't do it if it weren't with you. You got it all taped, eh Sniff? You're the man. I know you and the law, that's why I trust you."

Sniff allowed himself a smile at the tangled logic.

"Ok, Eric, as it happens, I don't just think you're on to something. I know it. You seen the supermarket deliveries around here – they need a tanker, not a van. How much, though, Eric? How much can you get and how much is it? And I want to meet the suppliers in person, Ok?"

Two days later, three men from a town in South Wales that Sniff had never heard of turned up in Eric's car park.

"It's good stuff, mate," declared a gangly, heavily tattooed man in his mid-thirties and who looked unlikely to see his mid-fifties. His name was Dave. "And you don't need any more than that, Ok?"

Roskosh Premium Vodka, triple distilled. Russia's finest. It looked like the real thing. Sniff declined a tasting.

"Ok," said Sniff, "what else you got? Is it just vodka, or do you have any other special offers?"

Gangly Dave looked furtive. "Me and my colleagues, well, we are talented, isn't it – we'll get what you want; you just tell us what it is. Or, if you've got something or someone you need sorting, we'll do the sorting as well. We're bloody good at it, I can tell you. No one ever knows nothing. Invisible when we're working, that's us."

Sniff was sold. Here was a way to sort out Dan and his 'tart'. Right in front of him and comfortably distant. He took Dave by the shoulder and led him away from Eric.

"As it happens, I do have a little job you might like. There's a man who's fucked me up big-time and needs to put right. Nothing permanent, just long-term painful. Arms and legs. You know the story."

Dave knew the story all too well; he had grown up with it. At home, at school, on the streets, Dave saw violence everywhere. He had suffered from it, and he had benefitted from it. He had been hurt, and he had hurt others. For Dave, violence was routine. He had learned from his father, who was always ready to fight anyone he thought had crossed him. Dave's father was a fighter, but Dave's mother was a soft, kind, loving mum, and the only violence Dave could not countenance was that against women. Dave had his principles.

"First off," said Dave, "You give me a photo of the er, customer and a location. I'll do the rest. You give the money to

Eric, in cash obs. Tidy?"

A productive afternoon thought Sniff as he left The Carps with two deals done.

23

Adversity has the power to make relationships more abiding, with an impregnability, a depth that goes beyond the mind and into the soul. Home from their essential escape to the country after the trial's aftermath, Dan and Jo had become inseparable, even when they were apart. They would marry, Spray would celebrate their union as best man and Max had volunteered to arrange the stag night in Spray's absence.

Max and Dan had found amity after the trial, not just because Max had so openly given his support to Dan, and not just because he had done what Dan believed to be a great job at keeping the business flourishing in his absence. It was more, the two of them had discovered an affinity based on similar views and values.

Dan was unaware of Max's duplicity.

Max was acutely aware of his deceit and felt guilt and a hint of shame for the first time in his life. On the other hand, since Sniff's dramatic upturn in demand, he had been making thousands of pounds each month simply by handing over poly bags from goods inwards to Duggie's old Ford.

Dan had shared his concerns about drugs getting into his offices, and Max had, quite honestly, said he didn't know who was selling to Onetelcall UK's personnel. He knew Sniff thought he was dealing, skimming off some powder and selling it on, and that was where his Slicko nickname had come from, but he wasn't, and now he most certainly wouldn't.

It was when Dan offered Max a promotion to be his second-in-command that Max's conscience finally shrieked at him. He liked and admired Dan and he liked and enjoyed Jo's company. He hated Sniff and felt sorry for Duggie. He was terrified of Spray. If dilemmas had horns, this one was a ceratopsian dinosaur. Should he come clean? Should he do The Right Thing?

Should he just run away? He could certainly afford to run away now; he'd been banking his illicit thousands, and it now amounted to a significant sum.

Fate made his mind up, as it so often had.

Dan, not usually a vengeful or resentful man, had been moved to dreaming of comeuppance, of legal or illegal retribution for what Sniff had done to his beloved Jo. He had thought of hiring some muscle, but he couldn't countenance such cowardice. He had thought of going to the police but knew, as soon as the thought crossed his mind, that it would be an endeavour of futility.

It was reading the daily papers online that gave him the solution. In the publications that allow readers' comments, he was amazed by how cruel, inhuman, unfeeling, self-righteous and arrogant so many, often anonymous or pseudonym-protected, readers could be. They comment, he thought, with an assumed asperity that distinguishes the foolish and uninformed.

Like many of his more technical colleagues in Onetelcall, he knew more about hacking than most. Between them, they also knew about all of the common social media platforms, how they work, how the trollers work, how the political and subversive influencers operate and how campaigns can undermine elections, economies, companies and people.

Dan met Max in the Hunt Bar of the Royal George.

"Max, this conversation isn't happening, Ok? I am going to suggest something which you may not like or approve of. If that's the case, a bit like Jo's courtroom revelation, you can't unhear it, but I hope you'll forget it and forgive me. If you are not so virtuous and think I'm on to something, then I'd very much appreciate your help."

Max was intrigued and alarmed. Was Dan about to share a plan to catch the trafficker? Oh shit. He was about to try some gun-spiking, but Dan was speaking again.

"It's about that bloody Sniff character, can't tell you how

much he sticks in my craw and, please understand this, I want to get back at him for attacking Jo and for everything she had to go through in the trial, all because of him. Max, I want him hung out to dry, I want him to suffer, I want to break him, and I think I know how to do it. Are you with me so far?"

Max was not just with him, he was ahead of him. Of course, he'd support Dan in any enterprise, but he could see with sudden clarity that his two worlds were about to converge with a mighty crash. Any plan which brings Sniff down could be his undoing too. He had no choice now but to go with the flow.

"Dan, you know I'm with you regardless. I gotta tell you that going after Sniff may bring up some surprises you won't like, but don't let that stop us now, what's your plan?"

Dan explained in more detail than he knew he'd evolved. Talking makes it real, and he filled in obvious gaps in the plan as they became apparent during his explanation.

"Clever, Dan. That's clever. It isn't illegal, is it? The only ones who get hurt are the bad guys, and Sniff will be royally buggered without anyone laying a finger on him even though he deserves a right good kicking if you ask me. Are you going to tell our glorious leader about this?"

One door shuts, they all slam, thought Max. If Sniff goes down and Spray knows about it, I am in for the chop without question. He was trapped, and he knew it.

"You know something, Max? I've known Spray for a long time now. He's been my best chum and a brilliant colleague and boss. Technically, he's gifted; business-wise, he's way ahead of so many smart techies. I like him and admire him but, just lately, I'm beginning to wonder if I can truly trust him. He's been very odd, very dismissive about some of my suggestions for cracking down on any drug action in the company. Could just be me getting older and more suspicious, but I think, just this once, I might keep Spay out of the loop. It's a private thing, not a Onetelcall issue, so I'm not under any obligation to keep him informed, and if, for any reason, he came down against the idea, I'd be stuck because I'm not letting Sniff off, not for anything."

"Let me think about this too, Dan. I'm pretty hot, not that I should say this to you, on the workings of some of the darker boards and rooms in the hidden depths of the web, I may be able to add a little extra value to your plan. Let me have a look, and shall we meet here again, same time tomorrow?"

Max was agitated and tense. He beat up his Audi all the way back to his flat, where he poured himself an industrial-sized whiskey and drank it quickly. Oh, fuck it, Max, what to do? he asked himself. The whiskey warmed him and, slowly, began to mellow his thoughts. He looked at himself in the mirror.

What sort of person are you? he asked the refection. What sort of person do you want to be? Is it to be an illegal, sybaritic life or an honest, poorer existence? What shall I do? Is this the time I choose how my life will be? Is this my Rubicon moment?

He opened his laptop. He knew the brave alternative would be to address Dan face-to-face, speak the truth, and admit his malefaction directly. The less courageous route would be the written word. It would be more explanatory and safer from sudden attack when the facts hit the fan.

"Dan, I have to admit this before we go any further," he typed, "I am not the good guy I think you think I am. I am guilty of so much. Now is the time for me to confess and for you to decide the consequences."

Once he'd started writing, the words were a torrent, like tears of absolute sorrow. The catharsis was overwhelming; the guilt would be life-changing.

"You were worried that I might not approve of your plan for revenge on Sniff, that I might not approve or judge you. My admission is so much worse, and you will be appalled. It will be up to you what you do about it. Turn me in or understand and help me make amends. I don't know, but I can't go on without confessing to you. If we go after Sniff together, we'll be putting ourselves in some danger, and I don't want to be the surprise weak link in your chain."

With that preface, Max continued his statement of revelation. He described how he'd met Spray, how Spray had recruited him and threatened him, how Spray was protective of Dan, but how dangerous he could be. He described the drug traffic flow via Duggie and Sniff. Max was forthright in his self-condemnation. He was, he acknowledged, selfish and greedy. He was easily, perhaps willingly, manipulated. He had only recently understood what remorse could mean.

He was about to email his mea culpa missive but paused. He thought about Spray's choice of the written word in a letter and saw its sagacity. He printed out his document and, while those without a restless conscious slept, Max quietly popped his envelope through Dan's letterbox.

Dan had spent the next day making a new business presentation and arrived at the Royal George a little late and still full of the adrenalin that high-level presentations gave him. He'd read and reread Max's statement. He was glad that his day had been so filled, so pressured, that he hadn't had time to think about it too deeply. Now, as he walked into the Hunt Bar, he was wondering what he'd say, wondering just what his thoughts were.

He had, of course, talked it over with Jo, without telling her why he was in such conversation with Max or about his plans for Sniff's future. In subjects of morality and conscience, Jo was more pragmatic than the on-off, right-wrong, black-white Dan. She blamed this thinking on the ones and zeros of his technical education.

"Christ Dan," she said after reading Max's letter, "that took some guts; he must think the world of you, perhaps a bit for me too, to do this. He must trust you a lot too. You could have him arrested on the spot with this, he must know that, so he must believe you'd see why he thinks you won't shop him. And you won't, will you? You'll give him a hard time for a short time and then figure something out for the best. Won't you, Dan." It wasn't a question, it was cognisant empathy.

Max was waiting on a bar stool, pallid and strained; he'd had a difficult day. Minor problems had been insurmountable. Simple questions had been intrusive. A phone ring was enough to make him jump. Tension showed in his eyes. Oddly, Dan wanted to tell Max about his day. He'd done well, even by his own self-critical standards, and a juicy new project was all but his, another win for Onetelcall. Buoyant and elated, Dan looked at Max and smiled. It was a smile that put a plug in the hole at the bottom of Max's world.

As they walked side-by-side, drinks in hand to a small corner table, Dan sounded comforting when he said,

"Dear God, Max, you have been some sort of an idiot, haven't you? What are we going do to?"

Max tried to nod and shake his head at the same time. His grin was thin, as if in pain.

"Dan, I don't know what to say. I've told you everything, and there's no going back now. You decide. I know what I've done, and I know what I want to do about it long term, but, right now, I want to help you and Jo, otherwise, I'd never have admitted all this crap. But I can't tell you what to think, how to react, what to do next. Up to you, mate, it's up to you," Max shrugged helplessly.

Dan looked stern. "What you've done is bad. What you've enabled is so much worse than bad; that shit kills people. You know it does. That makes you just about guilty of manslaughter. You've profited from the vile trade of those trafficking scum; you've made lots of money from people's pathetic addictions and broken lives. You've been, by your own admission, weak and greedy, but worse, you've buried your humanity under your hedonism, and I'm not sure yet if it can recover from that smothering."

Max was even paler and now sweating slightly. He turned slightly in his seat, looking at the door as if expecting the drugs squad to burst in with guns and dogs. He knew how meaningless protestations of change could sound, no matter how heartfelt. He looked at Dan in silence. No trite answers, no pleas, no contrition, no anguish would suffice.

"I have asked you to help me in something which, if not illegal, is certainly reprehensible to most people. You damaged lives at a distance, and I'm proposing to damage a life, deliberately and harshly, at first hand. I'm arguably just as bad, and I'd certainly be hypocritical to judge you now. So, where do my morals stand? Do I need your help more than I need to offer you up to whatever justice our police and courts feel they should dish out? Have you done more or less damage than many an undercover police officer? Are you a sub-human drug dealer or a fallible fool who might yet do more good than, so far, he has done harm? Most of all, do I trust you, can I trust you?"

Max felt a little stronger, a little more confident.

"You've got to know that, as far as you are concerned, I'm totally trustworthy. I told Spray Wilson I'd never stand by and see either of you come into any danger or harm's way. I have plans for making amends, for salving my conscience, I suppose by using the money I made to help people like those whose habits made it for me in the first place. But you must believe me, Dan, there's nothing I'd like to see more than Sniff and his band of trash get what they deserve," he paused for a moment, "except for that little Duggie character, Dan. I feel sorry for him, he's not one of them, they just use him horribly and callously; I'd like to help him if I can."

They talked until the bar closed. They discussed morals and honesty. They discussed traditional justice and 'street' justice. They pooled what they knew about Sniff, about Spray, about the size of the drugs business in Olderbury. They talked about the destructive potential of an adroitly devised social media campaign. They talked, planned, plotted and drank. They shared a taxi to their homes.

24

One of the effects of the pandemic was a surge of social media pressure groups and waves of wokism, the awakening of the uninformed and unaware in matters of inclusivity, diversity and gender. Woke activism was driven by social media. Originally simple platforms for students to stay in touch, social media grew into the 2000s and then exploded into a wild west of unattributable opinion, bullying, forceful minority views, intimidation and threat, personal attack and destruction. Social media was hijacked and manipulated from being a friendly communication conduit to a politicised, weaponised tool of multiple forms of war.

Soon enough, cracks appeared. Some of the global movements for race or gender were shown to be insidious incursions from eastern countries. Marxist-inspired disingenuous movements made their founders wealthy whilst thousands upon thousands of unquestioning idealists believed the misinformation the platforms spread with malice.

Dan and Max had followed the trajectory of social media from harmless to destructive and watched in horror as worldwide racial tension was fuelled by demagogic, dissembling faux anti-racialism propaganda. They were both very aware of the dangerous power of social media. They had seen it used to attack their corporate clients and to end the careers of senior businesspeople and politicians. False accusations, mining of ill-advised historic social media posts, fake news and imagery were the simple tools of online assassins. To offer an unpopular opinion was to be cancelled, ostracised and irrevocably blighted.

Troll farms proliferated around the world, notably in Russia, China, Albania, Turkey and India. For money, power, political interference, territorial aggression, state-sponsored attack, personal destruction, and ideological influence, for so many nefarious purposes, banks of well-paid hackers and trolls were on hand to spread their form of connected devastation. Traditional wars had been fought with guns; traditional scores settled with muscle. In the 21st century, only provincial, low-grade drug dealers used guns and knives; contemporary thugs and warriors used keyboards and video-fake tools.

Onetelcall had an extensive database of trolling, hacking, and subversive online techniques in its combined intelligence resource. Dan and Max scoured it. Max researched the darker areas of the web. It didn't take long for them to sufficiently ameliorate their already expert knowledge to feel fully prepared, proficient, and ready for the fray.

The first chore had been to gather mobile phone-captured video of Sniff in as many locations and circumstances as possible. One of Max's conquests, a girl called Ruby, a videographer by profession, was cajoled by Max into going undercover for this purpose. She had hidden her natural good looks with a wig, glasses and almost theatrical make-up. Dressed in a nondescript coat, she tailed Sniff for several days and delivered sequences that Max and Dan thought exceptional. She enjoyed the thrill of the game as much as the envelope full of cash with which Max rewarded her.

Deepfake, synthetic media, popular in character assassination, revenge porn, commercial porn and political corruption, really did put words in peoples' mouths. Using readily available deepfake apps, creative editing enabled realistic, highly believable video to be produced from any clips and sequences; totally false, totally plausible.

Dan and Max's first targets were the standard, commonly popular, high-use social media platforms. They opened multiple spurious home pages in Sniff's name. They used comment propagation tools to plant opinions and remarks on as many user pages as possible. They broke into online conversations to put Sniff into forums and network discussions. In a week, Sniff was as prominent on social media as some minor celebrities.

They posted videos of him selling, snorting, injecting himself, beating up a young girl, deriding his customers, drinking to excess, evidently colluding with a couple of police officers and making vile comments about disabilities, ethnicity, gender-fluidity and poor, needy or segregated people in general. They threw in a clip of Sniff swearing about his mum for good measure. The lip-synch and voice were perfect. Ruby's new boyfriend, a part-time voice-over artist from the video production house she worked for, was thrilled to play along in the 'experiment,' although he didn't understand the full implications of what he was doing.

It worked. It worked faster and better than either Dan or Max had expected. In days, people were pointing at Sniff in the streets, avoiding him or hurling abuse at him. Small groups followed him around town, to his flat and the pubs. His multiple online presences attracted vitriol and hate. Sniff was cancelled. Without warning, his life had fallen apart, leaving him with no recourse, no defence.

In two weeks, he went into hiding. Arfa and Lardy considered their options and 'did a fuckin' runner while we've still got both legs.' Olderbury's drug supply dried up, and none of the neighbouring dealers would risk filling the void. Burgerman decided to sell up; the barber moved onto prescription painkillers he extorted from his sister, a nurse, and Biggabookie's John Mayhew just shrugged and went on, as usual, skimming where he could. Duggie was bemused and suddenly very lonely again.

The police adopted a no-comment stance when questioned about the sudden decline in drug-taking in the town. Olderbury News ducked the story altogether as it was just too difficult to report. The Chief Inspector had toyed with the idea of claiming credit for a covert operation but knew it would never stand up to scrutiny, so he stuck with a professional, knowing, no-comment.

Sniff had made his way west, to Wales. Eric's voddy mate Dave knew a flat in Caldicot. It was safe, and nobody in the area would grass him up. Dave didn't do computers and couldn't understand what Sniff's problem was. Nor did he care. Arrogant arsehole reduced to mere arsehole, he thought. He'd make more money out of the man, and that was what mattered.

The flat's sitting room featured an old plastic leatherette black sofa and a TV the size of a small cinema, nothing else. Here, Sniff, accompanied by a bottle of Dave's vodka, gloomily reviewed his plight. He didn't know how he'd done it, but he was sure that Dan was behind this public demolition job. His hatred of Dan and, by association, Jo became obsessional. He may be finished in Olderbury, but he'd still have his revenge; those two would pay a terrible price, he promised himself.

"Here y'are Dave," Sniff said, handing over a stiffened envelope, "them photos you wanted, one of the fuckin' bastard Dan and one of his fucking floosie bitch Jo. You got their address at home and at work in there too. Should be all you need innit? And, what I said about just arms and legs. Well, he's fuckin done me up, right and proper. I'm totally fuckin screwed now, that's why I'm here innit, so I want him to fuckin hurt, know what I mean, really fuckin hurt, her too."

Dave looked at his client. He didn't like what he was hearing. A magistrate had described him as a recidivist with some principles, and he liked that. He had principles alright, and he was very principled about not hurting women. He had principles about being paid too. Taking the envelope, he said,

"It'll be three of us, that's a monkey each, so fifteen hundred quid in all, Ok? And I don't hurt women. I don't like being asked to do that. Don't ask me again, Ok? And I ain't been paid for the last lot of vod; Eric says he can't pay me 'cos you haven't given the money from what you sold. Is that right? I want that too, Ok?"

Sniff squirmed. "Yeah, yeah, you'll get your fuckin money all right, soon as the job's done."

Dave jumped in, "Oh no mate, before, I want my money before I do anything, none of your half and half, you want me to do a job, you pay me first, and I do the job. That's what it is, isn't it? I told you straight off, you'd have paid Eric, but now you're here, you pay me direct."

Sniff nodded his agreement. "Tell yer what, I'll come with you. It'll be night; no one will see me. I'll get my money and give it to you on the spot, both lots, the muscle and the voddy; how's that?" Dave took his turn to nod.

When he was briefing his two accomplices, Dave said, "Either of you on this social media stuff, seen what all the fuss about Sniff is about?"

One of them, Darren, tapped on his mobile, the screen lit up with moving images. It showed faked video of Sniff seeming to beat up a young girl, followed by a scene of him aggressively berating his mother.

Dave's look darkened, his eyes squinted. "Maybe a bit of a change of plan here, boyos," he said quietly.

25

Jimmy and Margarita ordered drinks from the butler in their exclusive Loft Suite of the K Tower hotel in the cosmopolitan area of Tijuana. They were worried. Business from the UK had bombed without warning. Spray didn't know what was happening. Word had reached Dordrecht and Strasbourg that the UK was in some sort of trouble, and both locations had gone dark.

They knew, and Spray knew, what Dan and Max, Karl and Chloe couldn't know. The 'gear' distributed via Onetelcall wasn't the whole story, Spray had set up background networks in each country as insurance, and those too were reacting to rumours of there being trouble.

"We've got to prioritise Mago," said Jimmy, using an affectionate name for his cousin, "because this is very real trouble for us and the family. If business in Europe takes a hit because Spray's distribution chain is compromised, it will be us and our family who feel the pain, and I'm not going to let that happen, that's for sure. So, we gotta act hard and fast. Prioritise, that's what we gotta do."

"I see matters very clearly, cousin, and I say this. First off, you must go to Europe now, today and meet the redundants, convince them of their duty and get them going at full speed again. You must make sure there are no loose ends, that is our very first priority, and we will keep our family safe from any disciplinary action our partners may want to hit us with."

Jimmy thought about her advice. The 'redundants' was Spray's techie reference to redundant systems, or mirror systems Onetelcall often installed as fail-safes for their customers. It described the emergency backup role of distribution routes he and Jimmy had created in London, Rotterdam and Marseilles. Each region was run by a known family friend and, while more expensive, was efficient and trustworthy. He knew he could switch them on instantly and, although profits may be dented in the short term, they wouldn't plunge to the extent that family business partners would seek recompense in their favoured form of drive-by shooting.

"Then," continued Margarita, "if we leave him where he is, Spray will be a dead man before the week is out. Our partners know about him and his role in the organisation. For sure, they will blame him, as well as us, for any fuck-ups in Europe. They probably already know what's going down in Olderbury, and I'd bet the people over there already have contracts against them, probably hits by the old Guadalajara guys or our friends here in Tijuana."

Again, Jimmy agreed. "Where're you at Mago? With Spray, I mean? You know the choices. We take him down, which isn't an option for me, we leave him for the other groups to waste, or we get him out and hide him. If we pull him out, you'll have to do it while I'm in London. But think Mago, think where you will take him because once he's gone, you'll have to hide too. It's up to you of course, but you might want to run off together and make a new life while you've both still got a chance?"

Margarita looked at her cousin, her eyes revealing the emotion she suddenly felt. She had no way of knowing if she genuinely loved Spray because she'd never really felt love. She did know she'd rather be with him than without him. For now, that seemed more than good enough.

Jimmy could read her thoughts.

"This is what I think, Mago. I think you and Spray have a connection, you understand one another in a world where nobody else would understand either of you, except me, of course, but I don't matter here. Spray has no choices but to disappear; you have some choices but not so many as you might think. You know the people we have as partners; you've just mentioned two of them, they'll put a knife in your ribs just for having been seen with Spray in the past, and there are many,

many photographs of you two together aren't there? Once we thought we'd need them to keep Spray in line, now they could be death warrants."

Margarita nodded; she had seen people killed for much less.

"Not even you know this, Mago, but I tell you now that I have a place on Rio Guayllabamba near Quito in Ecuador. Nobody, that is nobody but you now, knows about it. It has a hidden floatplane mooring; it is safe, concealed, and has better than state-of-the-art defences throughout the property and the eighty hectares surrounding it. There is no trace back to me, the family, the business, nothing. It is my ace, my sanctuary, and the farmland grows good cacao, not coca. It's yours, for you and Spray, if you want it. Take the right precautions and you will be safe for the rest of your lives with all the money you need. No more family business, no more risk, and, I hope, no more violence. You might even have…"

"Stop, stop, stop," cried Margarita, sobbing and smiling at the same time. Her arms were wrapped tightly around Jimmy, her face pressed to his shoulder. "I can't… I can't take all this from you. It's yours, and you may need it in a hurry one day. I just can't…"

"You can and you will. Los Golandrinos, that's what it's called, isn't my only secret hideaway; I've always known that exile would be my future, so I've made many plans. I have many identities, I've piled up more money than that old Greek king, and I may well take an extended vacation after this Europe trip too. You know, I may not be safe from retribution or revenge, but that's Ok, I wanted out anyway, it's been great, but it's getting too deadly now, too many hoodlums are taking control, too many politicos, too many mad people who kill for the sake of it."

Margarita was making plans even as her protestations continued. She would hire rental cars for the drive, in stages, from Tijuana to Ohio, different names, different licences, different credit cards; she'd be untraceable. Then they'd fly Spray's Cessna in unlogged legs from Ohio to Quito. She'd call in favours from trusted family friends in Charlestown, Miami, Gun Bay on Grand Cayman, Managua and Medellin, Colombia for unregistered landings. They'd fly the three thousand or so miles over a week, staying over at each leg breakpoint for rest, food, fuel, and to make sure they couldn't be followed or tracked. They'd disconnect the plane's open systems, and they'd even throw away their mobile phones to use nameless sim-only burners. Invisible in full flight.

She laughed, cried, shouted and whispered through her plans with Jimmy who, with a few useful additions of safety, such a pistol, an RF jammer, some more false identities, enthusiastically approved. Jimmy also arranged for a new transponder and false aircraft number graphics to be delivered to K-Hotel for Margarita to take to Spray.

Margarita's only worry now was that Spray might not be as compliant as her plans demand. He might not want to be with her. He might not want to go into a life of expatriation or isolation, and he might not want to run at all, to leave his beloved company. He may have his own plans to go to Europe and sort out his mess. She shared her worries with Jimmy, who, as usual, was well ahead of her. He tapped the mobile phone speed dial. Spray answered immediately.

"Hey Jimmy, I've been expecting your call, "Spray's voice sounded strained and taut.

"Hey buddy," responded Jimmy, trying to sound lighter than he felt, "seems the world is turning into a pile of shit, eh? What's going down in the UK? Crazy man, just crazy. The whole damn thing has gone fubar and there's going to be some heavy, like really heavy repercussion, you know that, I know you know that. Where are you at, man?"

"Jimmy, all I know is that Dan, my top man in Europe, has done a real number on the Olderbury distributor, and now the whole network is imploding throughout the UK, and it's spread to France and the Netherlands too. Seems Dan and Max have run a massive social media hatchet job, and it's making real big waves; don't know where it's going to end, but I do know blood will flow, I just know it."

"You got any plans Spray? You figuring out how to rescue the situation? Me, Margarita and the family, well, we're all picking up the shockwaves from your region's fuck-up. Our partners are probably tooling up as I speak. Your man Dan and your new operator Max have screwed us big time, they may not have intended to, and I don't think they did, but the reality is we are dead if we don't act like right now."

"Jimmy, this is no time for false heroics or empty boasts. I just didn't see any of this coming and, right now, I don't know, I've no clue what I can do to fix it. I thought about hot-footing it to London but, by now, I might be walking straight into a cell; the UK police must be all over this by now.

"I'm trying to think about ways of keeping Dan out of the shitstorm, but I just can't see a way. And, Jimmy, I gotta tell you, I'm worried too. This whole fucking disaster has come from nowhere and has created havoc in the network. I can get to Marseilles and Rotterdam in no time to fire up the redundants for sure, but my biggest worry, and I must say this, my biggest worry is that your family partners will finger me as the fall guy and I'm in line for a shiv in the back."

"That's how we read it, too, buddy. Me and Margo – Margarita – we've been doing some talking and we've got a plan. I'm saying no more. I'm not saying anything on this phone or any other, you understand? But I'll ask you this, just once. Do you trust me and Margarita?"

"Yeah, Jimmy, you know I do. Both of you."

"OK, just know that we got a long-term, long-distance plan, and once you're in, there isn't an out. Say yes, and it is goodbye to everything you have, everything you know. Say no, and you'll hear nothing from either of us again." Jimmy played all his cards.

"Then I say 'yes' Jimmy; what do I have to do?"

"Nothing other than be ready, tie up loose ends, plan what

you have to plan, leave what you have to leave and wait. That's all I can say, but here's a last word from my cousin, hang on."

"Hey, Spray," said Margarita, taking the phone from Jimmy, "oh, hey Spray. This is for real, and it's right for you and right for me. I never said anything like this before, and I haven't said anything now, but you know what I mean. Wait Spray, just wait and be ready."

26

Usually a quiet man, Dave was now monosyllabic and showed a face his two mates, Darren and Ivan, hadn't seen before. It was dark, frowning and hard. The three of them travelled, side-by-side, in the front of the Transit. Sniff had been given an old mattress to soften his journey in the back of the van. He had objected,

"Oi you fuckers, I'm fuckin' paying for all this, I ain't goin' in the fuckin back!"

Commuter traffic filled the motorway; cars and vans tailgated in the outside lane while the middle and inner lanes were almost empty. Dave, always careful not to stand out, kept to a steady 55mph on the inside lane.

"Ere," said Darren over the sound of Radio 2, "you dun 'arf hate this bloke we're going after doncha, why's that then?"

"None of your fuckin business is it," replied Sniff, still angry about being bundled into the back. "All you gotta know is that he's getting what he fuckin deserves, and that's that. He fucked me about right and proper, the wanker. My boys Lardy and Arfa have had to bugger off, and my driver Duggie daren't leave his flat, all because of that tosser and his slicko fuckin mate. I want them both to see the error of their ways, know what I mean?"

"Got ya," replied Darren, "we're alright with that, ain't we, Ivan. Me and Ivan got a bit of previous on lesson-teaching."

Ivan laughed loudly.

"Dave said you wanted us to give his bird a little slap an' all, that right?" asked Darren.

"Well," replied Sniff warily, picking up on a tone of voice, "she fuckin had me in court, didn't she, lied and wiggled and tarted her way out of fucking stabbing me didn't she, bitch, so yeah, I'd thought about her being put straight but yer man Dave said he wasn't on for that, so that's that, Ok by me I suppose, but she's still a fuckin bitch tart."

"My mate Ivan, well, he's a bit of a computer buff, ain't ya Ivan?"

Ivan laughed loudly.

"He says he's seen you on them social sites, doing drugs and all that and being a bit of a tough guy yourself."

"It ain't fuckin true, it's a fuckin tuck-up isn't it, that wanker and his mate, it was them what put all that stuff on the internet and its screwed me good and proper but it ain't fuckin real, none of it, it's all fuckin bollocks, made up, not real, make-believe bollocks, honest it is."

"So, what ya think about hitting women then, eh? Is that stuff all bollocks as well, I mean, you did want us to tap the girl, didn't you?"

Sniff could see Dave's shoulders square up behind the wheel and began to worry.

It was dark by the time they reached Olderbury. Dave parked away from the lights in the most hidden part of The Carpenters Arms car park. He knew that a couple of local police kept an eye on the pub, but he was sure they didn't go as far as taking vehicle numbers, and he was just as certain that Eric's CCTV wouldn't be available if required.

"I'm not sure I want to go in there," said Sniff, knowing that his infamy had not evaded his very short list of friends.

"S'up to you innit," said Dave thinly, "we need a bit of fuel, me and my boys, don't we?"

"Too fuckin right," came the joint reply.

Sniff looked around the car park and noticed an S3 Audi. He recognised it.

"Nah, I ain't fuckin goin in am I, that car there, that car

belongs to Dan's bloke Max, and he's one of ours tonight, he's due for a kickin' tonight, and I don't want him to see me do I."

"S'up to you," repeated Dave as he walked towards the pub, "I'll get Ivan to bring you a pint and some crisps, like being a kid again, eh, except for the pint… or not, I dunno."

Max had decided to call in just out of interest. He knew that it was an occasional field office for Sniff, and he wondered what the word in the pub might be now that the social media campaign had done its work.

Eric was taciturn. No, he hadn't seen Sniff. No, he hadn't seen Duggie. No, he wasn't going to talk about anything.

"You want a drink or what?"

Max asked for a gin and tonic, and Eric looked disapproving. As his drink chinked its way across the bar, Max noticed three men walking in. He hadn't seen them before, but then he didn't visit the Carps that often. They looked unpleasant and agitated. Max felt a chill of apprehension, which became a shiver as he looked out of the window just in time to see Sniff, yes it was Sniff, sneaking into the back of a big, old grey van.

Max swallowed his drink and left the pub. He had to find Dan and let him know that Sniff was back and had, perhaps, bought some rental muscle with him.

Dave watched him leave, guessed his mission and motive and turned his attention back to his drink, plenty of time yet.

At around the same time and only a short distance away, a Hertz Dream Collection Aston Martin DB11 convertible parked, with no attempt at modest discretion, in the Royal George hotel car park. Two immaculately tailored men stood up from the car, adjusted their sunglasses and walked into the hotel to check into their reserved rooms. Neither man was well known, and it was better that way. Those who knew them knew them as Jesus and Angel, which was their correct original given names and not adopted names to advertise the ungodly nature of their business.

Angel and Jesus had taken the scenic route from Chihuahua, via Mexico City, Los Angeles, Singapore, Kuala Lumpur, Dubai and eventually, Heathrow. Anyone determined enough could have tracked them, but so far in their extensive history of such convoluted international travel, no one had tried or bothered. They had a terse and uninformative brief. Go to the UK, find a town called Olderbury, find the local drug dealer and kill him. He is a crazy man who's created his fate on the internet. He puts the organisation in danger, go there, do the work, come home. Leave no trace. Do not buy girls, do not get drunk anywhere, do not drive on the wrong side of their roads.

A little later, after acting like confused tourists asking odd questions, Jesus and Angel found out most of what they needed to know about this lunatic Englishman. They didn't, as yet, know where to find the man but they had some clues. They would go to The Coopers Arms, they decided, as this had been suggested as one of their quarry's haunts. They would ask more questions. People would answer because they always did. It was always easy. They would be parking their rental sports car at Manchester Airport tomorrow evening, job done. They would take another series of flights, using more identity packs of credit cards, papers and passports. They would remain undetected because they knew how to avoid any law, all law.

Max drove away from The Carps and hit his in-car phone button to get through to Dan.

"Max, I wasn't expecting to hear from you tonight. Everything Ok?"

"Dan, hi, yes, er no, listen. Sniff right? I've just seen Sniff getting into the back of an old tranny in the Carps car park. I think he's got some gorillas with him, and I've got a bad feeling that he might be coming after you or us or, well, something, I don't know, but I think we should be on our guard."

"Ok, Max, let's stay calm. I'm surprised Sniff's showing his face around here and, as we've so often said, he must know it was us, or me at least, who pulled the S.M. stunt and that's more than reason enough to come for revenge. He's like that, isn't he? Look, I'm at Jo's at the moment; why not come over now, and we'll see what happens."

Dave finished his pint and asked Eric for a refill.

"You up here on business then?" asked Eric now that Dave's demeanour had softened a little.

"Yeah, doin' a job for Sniff, at least that's the plan. What do you reckon, Eric? This Sniff of yours. Is he Ok or is he what everyone else thinks he is, you know, like a bully and woman beater?"

"Well, he ain't no saint, never has been, and he's got a turn of nastiness in him, that's no lie. They reckon he grassed up one of his mates and had him banged up, you know. But he's always been Ok with me, so I shouldn't say stuff against him. I didn't know he'd fallen out with his mother, though she was a right skag from what I've heard; even when he was a kid, she was on the game, so what else can I tell you."

"Yeah, well, I've got no bind about him shifting gear, someone will always do it, and it might as well be him, but I don't like grasses and I don't like men who hit women but, most of all Eric, I don't think I like Sniff. I got principles, you know, even a magistrate told me that, and I might use a bit of that principle tonight."

Dave picked up his new pint and sipped thoughtfully. He had only half his money, so far, for tonight's work, so it wasn't, strictly speaking, a contract. That's a principle appeased then. Dave was rapidly forming the opinion that whatever tonight's mark had done, Sniff probably deserved. Stabbed by a girl? No, Dave didn't believe it. Something was wrong and he wasn't going to be used to deliver revenge when revenge wasn't deserved. Principles are principles.

"Ere, Dazzer, Ive, we should have a little chat. In a mo, we'll be back in the van off to do the job. Trouble is, I don't like this Sniff geez, I think he's a wrong-un. I told you he wanted us to smack a woman, and you know I don't like that. Well now, I know he grassed up a mate an' all, he's treated us like shit, and he's shy on the dosh. What do you two say?"

"Whatever you say, Dave," replied Darren, "we're with you and what you say is right by us. But seeing as you ask, I think Sniff is a snivelling little shit and, as you ask, I would mind giving him a little tap while we're at it."

Ivan laughed loudly.

"That's what I was thinking," said Dave. "We might do some of the job we said we'd do, but we might also catch Sniff in what you might call the crossfire."

Max parked his S3 on the street opposite Jo's flat, just where Duggie had parked all that time ago.

Angel and Jesus parked their ostentatious Aston Martin a street away from The Coopers; it was slightly longer than the width of the terraced house behind it and a lot more valuable. Dave drove his grey van to the back of the pub, where the car park was directly opposite the ground floor door to Jo's flat, the door which Sniff had hammered on that fateful night.

Sniff had an idea.

"Oi you lot, I've got a fuckin plan going on here, ain't I. First off, we knock out that fuckin CCTV camera over there," Sniff pointed at the camera which had so damned his evidence, "and then I'll go across the road, it'll bring back sweet memories," Sniff laughed.

Ivan didn't.

Dan and Jo held hands on the sofa as Max alternated between pacing and peeking through the window to the street below. For Jo, memories flooded back; a familiar tension and nausea gripped her again. Dan was calm on the outside but flutteringly panicky inside. He was a fit man but no match, he knew, for any contracted thugs. He felt trepidation at the prospect of being repeatedly punched, kicked and hit with whatever weapon may be to hand. Max was just pumped. He didn't let his imagination fuel any fear; all he thought was that if this was his chance to make some reparation, he'd seize it and fight like a demon for his friends.

He watched the Aston turn down the side street and slow down before going out of sight. He wondered who would risk parking a car like that in an area like this. Such thoughts left him the moment he saw the van turn into the Coopers' car park.

"Game on," he yelled, startling the already nervy Dan and Jo. "They are here. In the car park. Sniff and the three dudes." Max surprised himself by finding his description amusing. "Plan A it is then, let's do it."

Jo rang the police. She wondered what response she'd get. If any. Her call was answered; she began to explain.

Jo's doorbell sounded, and there was heavy knocking on the door. Even on the phone, Jo recognised the signature hammering. It all came back, but she stuck to her task of getting a rapid response from a care-worn call handler.

Jesus recognised his target the instant he saw a thin, slightly stooped man stride arrogantly across the road to a door. Jesus watched him as his fist struck the door with a rhythmic thudding. Angel opened his small alligator skin man bag and handed a precision weapon to his companion, keeping an identical pistol for himself. Both men got out of the car and sauntered up the road; they walked deliberately slowly, watching, waiting.

The front door opened and, reliving old experiences, Sniff moved to wedge his foot in the door to prevent it from being slammed shut again. He was wrong-footed because this time, the door was swung wide open, fast and hard, and Max roared out, shouting as loud as he could, fist-pumping away at his instant target. Not for the first time at this doorway, Sniff staggered backwards.

Darren and Ivan had been positioned on either side of the doorway and were now behind the charging Max. As Sniff fell back and Max pressed his attack, Darren and Ivan closed in behind Max. They both got a hand to Max's shoulders when Dan gave an almighty swipe with Jo's hockey stick and connected with both their heads.

Dave had been an onlooker, still wrestling with his principles. What he saw in Sniff's misguided attack was a coward, and Dave didn't like cowards either. Instead of backing up Darren and Ivan, Dave walked to the now stooping Sniff and twisted him around in an arm lock. Sniff, in shock, was now looking down the street where he could see four shiny black eyes coming towards him. Sunglasses? At night. What's that pop-pop sound?

Sniff hit the ground at Dave's feet. Blood was seeping from the corner of Sniff's mouth, and two red spots bled from his chest.

"Fuckin' 'ell," yelled Darren, "those two, there, look…" he pointed at Angel and Jesus as they stepped back into their car.

"They've only fuckin' shot him. Fuckin' 'ell. Shot him. They have. Shot him what the fuck…"

Jo stood at the door, the scene of her worst nightmare. This time there was a bizarre mix of panic and calm. What she saw next was amazing and, to her, quite surreal.

Max stood up, helped by his former attackers. Dave walked over to Dan, looked him solemnly in the eye and shook his hand. Within seconds, Dave, Darren and Ivan had gone. The Aston had long gone. Sniff was motionless on the floor but still moaning quietly. The sirens bought Jo back to reality.

27

It took fifteen months for Sniff to be found guilty of multiple charges, including drug trafficking, conspiracy and bribery. The CPS made a better fist of it this time and, although they dropped several more minor violence and lesser tariff misdemeanour charges, they mounted a prosecution case that resulted in an eighteen-year sentence.

When the judge delivered his verdict, Sniff wondered whether he'd have been better off being shot dead by the walking sunglasses. His early warning system had told him Dave wasn't to be trusted, and he'd taken the precaution of buying an online forty-nine, ninety-nine-pound stab vest. Instead of killing him instantly, bullets fired by Angel and Jesus were slowed and diverted by the vest. Even so, they had taken out one of his lungs and just missed his heart. Quick action by the ambulance team saved his life, and surgeons then ensured he'd be fit enough to serve every one of his years of incarceration.

After his introductory period, Kevin Sniff Taylor was sent to HMP Frankland, known as Monster Mansion. Rumours that Sniff had informed on a mate had reached the inmates and Sniff's first few months were an ordeal that took him to the edge of his endurance. They knew, in Monster Mansion, how to dish out long-term pain without the respite of unconsciousness. He spent a lot of time in solitary confinement for his protection.

While Sniff was on the operating table, Margarita changed her plans.

Forty hours of non-stop driving was too much; it would take too long. Without an urgent need to cover her identity for this first stage of her travel, she took a thirteen-hour flight to Cleveland, via Atlanta, where she hired a car. Sixteen hours after that last phone call, Margarita and Spray were together.

Spray was amazed at the power of his emotion; he'd never

felt it before. He suddenly knew that being with Margarita was what he wanted more than anything else. He had felt oddly dispassionate, as though he was watching himself from another world, as, during the sixteen hours of Margarita's journey, he made his preparations for a new life. He signed the stand-by disaster strategy documents of Onetelcall, making Dan its president and CEO. He transferred fifty per cent of his shares to Dan and put the remaining stock in a nominee account created in favour of Jimmy and the family. He said goodbye to his enterprise baby but, surprisingly, felt no sorrow.

It took Spray and Margarita over an hour to say hello. Afterwards, over a glass of wine, Margarita detailed her plan for their future life on Jimmy's ranch in Ecuador. Spray was overcome that Jimmy would do this for him, for them. He wanted to call, but Margarita pointed out the painful truth. From now on, they had to be on their guard. They were about to cease to exist as Spray Wilson and Margarita Lopez. No more casual phone calls, no more life as usual.

"You know, my love, that one day they will get us. One day we will be enjoying a quiet day in Quito when a motorbike will pass by, and we will be in holes. It will happen, I know it, but until it does, we must do two things; we must take great care and be vigilant against making simple, giveaway mistakes, and then we must ensure that we enjoy every day we have left."

Spray knew it too. His cold disengaged psyche had prevented him from understanding why his business with Jimmy and family could be seen as heinous in any way. Even now, as his inner feelings were being set alight by his relationship with Margarita, his empathy for addicts, for broken families, for drug-induced suicides and murders remained non-existent.

He did, however, feel a fraternal need to make some explanation to his innocent friend Dan. Yet again, he chose the written word.

'Dan, my old buddy,' he wrote. 'I owe you an explanation. We've been friends for so long, been through so much together and built so much that's good and worthwhile between us. Until the end, I don't think you ever suspected me of using the company for running gear. You'll be wondering why I did it. Well, old buddy, it's not been just for money, nor was it the only way I could fund the start-up. It was for excitement, the thrill, the same adrenalin fix I got from racing. I've let you down, and for that, I'm truly sorry.

I won't be there to be your best man, and I'm sorry for that too. You and Jo both deserve a good life and, perhaps, now I can make that happen. It's a wedding present and an apology in kind. Onetelcall is now yours. You'll have half of my shares plus all your own, which makes you king of the castle. Some of my stake goes to Jimmy and the family because I have to, but they'll never bother you again, I swear it. Just pay them their dividends, eh?!

You and Jo should come over here. My apartment is now yours too, so is my car and all the stuff. You don't get the plane, though. I need that, as you might realise.

I want to make it right for Max too. I used him and I leant on him. He may have been willing, but he was an innocent ready for manipulation, and that's what I did to him. Make him your replacement in Europe, will you? He's loyal to you; he'll serve you well and do a good job. I reckon he's learned a lot now. He's a bright kid, he just needed to understand what weakness and temptation can do.

You'll never hear from me or see me again, and that, my friend is the daddy of all bummers, but I have no choices. It was my making; I pay the price.

Make it happen, Dan, have a great life.

Spray, always your buddy.'

Spray ignored the prickling at the back of his eyes as he sealed and stamped the envelope.

Spray had already packed his life into the Cessna. Everything of value, including paintings, watches, uncut diamonds, currencies, bonds and crucial papers, were carefully placed in the hidden security holds of the modified aircraft. Even so, it took a further three hours to load Margarita's luggage from the hire car and then to disguise the 'plane, now for cloaked flight.

New decals, identification graphics, replacement radio modules and a new, false transponder were all fitted. Spray always kept the long-range fuel tanks topped up; the journey could begin from one life to another.

They were seized by the hysteria that comes from shock; it all seemed unreal. Excited, they giggled, whispered, clutched each other and felt high on the palpable tension and anticipation as Spray opened the throttles and the seaplane's floats left Ohio waters forever. Spray had mapped radar horizons all the way through to Grand Cayman, ensuring he could adjust height and direction to maintain invisibility, especially around refuelling points at Charlestown and the partner's waterside hangar near Miami. After ten hours flying time, two hours for fuel and three hours for a much-needed nap, the Cessna's floats made bow waves into a large creek just off Gun Bay, Grand Cayman.

Still feeling like eloping adolescents, Spray and Margarita gave themselves a day off. They slept a bit more but were too exhilarated to sleep for long. They headed to a shack bar on Rum Point and spent an afternoon eating shellfish and drinking Midori cocktails. More sleep and it was take-off time again, with a circuitous high and low course set for Managua.

In much less time than Margarita had planned, Spray shut down his plane's Lycoming engine and secured his mooring in the riverside water hangar of Jimmy's vast Ecuador haven.

"Oh Spray," murmured Margarita, "this is our home. How does that sound, eh? This is our first-ever home and likely our forever home too. Jeez, that's something, isn't it? We'll be safe here, my love. No one knows us, and nobody knows we are here except for Jimmy. Safe, at last," Margarita's words were part statement and part plea for reassurance.

Seventy miles away, at Quito airport, a matt black Airbus H125 helicopter, apparently registered to the Mexican Narcotics

Fighting Force, touched down. Two men, both in expensive back suits and wearing Dolce and Gabbana sunglasses, stepped out. No immigration queue for Angel and Jesus, who strode to a waiting car to take them sightseeing. They were looking for a man and a woman, and partner intelligence had a good idea of where they'd be.

"Si patron," said Angel on one of his mobile phones. "There are people on the rancho, it looks like them from this distance. Who else could be here, eh? You want that we go in closer?"

"It's them," came back a gruff voice. "Get a telephoto picture, understand? Get a picture of both of them, but from a distance, don't be seen."

"That's it, patron? You don't want that me and Jesus do, well, you know, do our work on them for you?" Angel touched the butt of his pistol.

"No Angel, no deaths today. That we know where they are is enough for now. One day we will need them. One day they will do what we ask of them. If they don't Angel, then you and Jesus can go to play."

28

Olderbury, now with a population of 46,700, was free from lockdown and restrictions. It had been a mixed story for the town. John Mayhew's betting business had boomed as gambling fever ripped through the ranks of furloughed workers who had spare money and nowhere to spend it. Individual losses rocketed, and unpaid accounts became a severe threat to Biggabookie' s liquidity. He had to temper avarice with commercial survival and imposed limits and checks on his punters. He had stayed away from any more drug dealing and felt better about himself for it. Perhaps ruining lives with just one addiction was enough for any man.

Burgerman became a victim of the drugs he so happily peddled. His habit grew and grew until he was a lost soul. His business closed down quite early into the first phase of Covid restrictions and, after collapsing in the street, he was admitted to intensive care and then referred for further addiction treatment.

As existing business withered, new enterprises sprang up. Veg-it-ate, vegan meal boxes delivered to your door, enjoyed a fad explosion of popularity that faded after a few months when the need for some succulent protein overcame the green ethics of some of the more reluctant converts.

The town's younger inhabitants found it tough. Away from school and college, isolated from friends, social media became even more essential for youthful communication.

As the Covid effect changed society throughout the country, social media became ever more vicious, vindictive and vitriolic. In Olderbury, younger users began to reject the constant harping and hectoring of great minority causes. They wanted to swap stuff, do jokes, laugh, share, and find sunshine on gloomy days. They didn't want, anymore, to be bullied into a sexual identity crisis, to find racism where none had previously existed, to save the planet while industrial nations around the globe spewed tons of poison into the air every second.

This rebound was not motivated by a lack of belief. Most of Olderbury's under twenty-fives were fervent in their views about gender understanding and support, about being fundamentally inclusive of race, creed and ability. They all cared deeply about the planet's future and did all they could to mitigate their individual contributions to its eventual demise.

The new editor of Olderbury News recognised this. Wendy Victor was a graduate in journalism from Portsmouth University and, after the usual two years of being 'the junior,' made it to chief reporter on the mixed media Shires UK Newsgroup. Her appointment as editor to Olderbury News upset the town's status quos.

Wendy Victor launched the 'We are Olderbury' online forum where there was something for everyone from gardening Q&A panels to the Supamegaplopotron page for kids. She used the printed media for follow-up news and in-depth features, and the online function catered for news as it happened. Cleverly, she attracted the younger generations, bringing them into the 'we-are' social media and encouraging them to share their honest thoughts and views about anything they cared to mention. It worked.

To begin with, the town council squealed in anguish at the change but, as time passed and tourists started to return, they began to understand how a new look Olderbury was, actually, very good for business.

She also published some probing and critical articles about policing in Olderbury with some retrospective analysis of how the town's drug consumption had ballooned so rapidly without check or sanction. The relationship between her predecessor and the Chief Inspector was not much of a secret and, like all gossip, had grown beyond reality. Wendy understood the exaggeration of rumour but still felt compelled to ask questions and publish facts and inconvenient truths Amongst her questions: why was Taylor not interviewed after the now-infamous Jo Hadge trial?

The Chief Inspector's cosy life became uncomfortable as he was scrutinised by teams working under the Deputy Chief Superintendent. The investigators invaded Olderbury nick and asked a lot of awkward questions about Kevin Sniff Taylor and his status as part-informer and part-criminal. The DCC's team also put Sergeant Peter Hamilton, DCI Clive Roberts and PC Amanda Cotter under pressure; they knew something was rotten in the nick of Olderbury, and the investigators wanted the rotters.

It was Sniff's former ally Clive Roberts who broke first. Ambitious and streetwise, he was not about to have his career prematurely terminated by protecting either his station boss or his former supplier. He had talked it over with Amanda.

"Don't know about you, Mand," he said, "but it seems to me we've got to be a bit clever now if we are going to get out of this with our careers intact. I know, and I do know, you are innocent in all this, but I've been a bit silly and, I have to say, the likelihood is that if I go down, so, probably, will you, justifiably or not. You know what the DCC henchmen- can you have henchwomen? Anyway, you know what they are like, it's all results and no concern about rights and wrongs."

PC Amanda Cotter looked coldly at her colleague and replied,

"You've not been silly, Clive, you've been a total tosser. You took gear off Sniff, and you kept quiet when you could have nicked him. I just don't get it with you and that vile bastard. Anything for a snort, is that it? Are you a druggie Clive, or are you a policeman in a bad disguise?"

"I'm not on the gear anymore, Mand, honest I'm not and, well, looking back, I know I've been a tosser, but I am a copper, and I want to be a good one, especially now when I've seen what bad policing can do, what damage it can create. I am, let me tell you, delighted that Sniff has got what he deserved. But Mand, seems to me that we've still left some shit on the street, and if we can clear it up, I reckon we'll save our necks and come out looking like fucking heroes."

"You mean Arfa and Lardy?"

"I do indeed, Mand, I do indeed and, if I'm more Maigret than Clouseau, then I reckon I know how to get a steer on finding them."

Amanda interrupted, "I've had a thought about that too, just as I was walking past Biggabookie and saw Mayhew a few days ago and thought that if it was him who put the word out to the drugs squad that Sniff was a big-ish dealer while he was in hospital, then he'll be a pushover for extracting more info now, and he'll know if anyone does, where those two slobs ran away to."

"Great minds, Mand, that's what I think too, and me and you ought to pay chummy Mayhew a little visit, eh?"

John Mayhew didn't need any interview tactics. He was more than willing to give up Arfa and Lardy; he disliked them both intensely as they loutishly swaggered and bullied under Sniff's protection.

"Try here," he said, pointing to an area just off Gravelly Hill, Birmingham. "That's roughly where they'll be; some relation of that fat bugger, I believe."

Clive and Amanda contacted the Erdington force. Their request for cooperation was welcomed on the proviso that they arrested only the two men they named. They didn't ask why but took what help they could get with gratitude.

Arfa and Lardy had fled to Birmingham because Lardy's cousin Mutley, nicknamed for his laugh, had a vacant bedsit just off the Tyburn Road in Erdington. Mutley was moving up in the world; his career was as an elder, running drug sales in various locations on the Tyburn Road and New Street, and his earnings had grown prodigiously through the pandemic. Mutley got them both involved on the street as watchers and stand-by muscle. Arfa and Lardy thought they were safe from any trouble from their previous lives with Sniff.

Local intelligence informed the two police officers from

Olderbury that two new older white men had been seen associating with known street-sellers around Canal Street and Erdington Hall Road; they'd be easy to spot amongst the range of more prevalent ethnicities.

After two days of pavements, it was Lardy who spotted allo-allo first.

"Fuckin' 'ell, Arf, it's that fuckin plod allo-allo innit, fuckin' look, it is it's only fuckin him and that girl-filth too. Oh fuck, Arf, they after us d'you think?"

Arfa looked and saw Clive and Amanda and a couple of local PCs walking towards him. He instantly knew they were done for, nicked, nabbed, buggered, screwed, and fully fucked. Of course, they could run, but not far or fast. They could fight but, with the amount of fed presence around them, they'd be flattened by a heavy weight of well-filled uniform in no time.

Very quickly, life changed for the two malefactors. They were taken to the West Midlands custody centre in Perry Barr, where they were held to face trial for offences committed in Olderbury and Birmingham. They would not feel freedom again for many years.

Clive and Amanda had outflanked the Birmingham drug squad task force which had been trying to break into the drug-dealer syndicates in that part of the city for months. Instead of being reprimanded for short-circuiting an active investigation, they both received commendations. Amanda requested a transfer to a drug investigation unit and became plain-clothes Detective Constable Cotter. Will Davies from Hedges & Co, solicitors, was one of the first to congratulate her; he'd known she'd make it.

29

Onetelcall, despite all the subterfuge and unseen disruption, continued its success. Dan and Max had enabled work-from-home for all employees whose jobs could be fulfilled in such a way. They were also, in their way, pioneering. They recognised the dangers of work-from-home regimes, the need for self-discipline, and self-motivation, the lack of close face-to-face contact and the loss of at-work fun times.

They motivated, they rewarded. They both spent time calling employees for a chat. They opened a company-wide on-demand, dip-in-dip-out teleconferencing system. They even introduced the Onetelcall page on 'We-are-Olderbury,' which kept users in touch and promoted a Onetelcall initiative to contact the town's elderly, lonely or less fortunate. Some techies grouped together to post mobile game coding challenges for home-bound schoolchildren, and soon, Supamegaplopatron became an online and mobile phone games producer. Whenever restrictions allowed, they arranged the best get-togethers they could achieve, and it was all very worth it, as performance figures would show.

When it dropped onto his hall floor, Spray's letter had a profound effect on Dan. Initial fury of betrayal subsided to anger at a lost-forever opportunity and friendship, which, in turn, gave way to sadness and a degree of understanding. For all that Spray had given him, Dan didn't feel any great gratitude. Perhaps he should, he thought, but he didn't.

Neither he nor Jo had missed Spray at their wedding. If it hadn't been for Spray, the whole Sniff tale of carnage might never have happened. Without Spray, how many people wouldn't now be suffering the agony of addiction? No, they didn't miss Spray at all. Even worse, they would now have to forgo their honeymoon as Onetelcall pressures on Dan meant no time off for him for a long time to come.

Before Spray's letter, Dan hadn't harboured any ambition to run the entire company. He was not about to move to America, and he had planned to slow down a little to spend as much time as he could with Jo, holidaying, playing and enjoying life. In truth, he felt a little dumped on. In the pre-letter days, he and Max, in fact, the whole company in all countries, had worked diligently to make Onetelcall a world leader in its field. Now everything had to change, but Dan wasn't sure he wanted to follow Spray's final edicts. He had other thoughts.

He talked about the future of Onetelcall with Max, without telling him about Spray's recommendation that Max runs the European regions. Since the night of his guilty revelation, Max had grown up. From the money he had made from Spray, he had made significant donations to addiction therapy facilities, none of which ever had enough funding and one of which, coincidentally, would be helping Burgerman into recovery.

As another act of atonement, of sympathy and hope, Max visited the Carps, now under new management as Eric and Peggy had retired to a static caravan home near Budleigh Salterton, to find Duggie and offer him a job, a proper, paid regular job in deliveries.

"Well, that's my plan," concluded Dan to Max. "What do you say? With Karl from Strasbourg and Chloe from Dordrecht, you will be the new management function. Of course, I'm still the boss, and final decisions are mine, for now anyway. The Ohio offices and production units will continue, but the UK will now be Onetelcall HQ. Makes sense all round."

"I want to say I don't know what to say!" Max laughed. "I'm your man, you know that. Karl, Chloe and I are a good team, really we are, and we're on a roll now anyway. Nothing can stop us, Dan!"

Dan smiled at his young colleague's obvious excitement and white-hot ambition. He glanced again at the brochure for a remote cottage by the sea and smiled even more.

"What's next then, boss?"

"A honeymoon, Max, a wonderful honeymoon. See you in a month. Don't call me."

———————————

About the Author

Tony has been writing for most of his life, from editing a group of newspapers to copywriting and creating speeches and scripts for global company videos and conferences.

His news and research instincts, combined with his interests in emerging technologies and new media, create the essence of his books which, although fictional, have a core of fact and real-life occurrences running through them.

Max deepfake revenge is his debut as an author. It involves the power of social media and technology, especially deepfake, and how it can be manipulated for crime and revenge. And in Tony's books, revenge is served with compelling extra heat.

Tony lives in Wiltshire with Sarah, his beloved wife and inspiration.

Available worldwide from
Amazon and all good bookstores

Michael Terence
Publishing

www.mtp.agency

www.facebook.com/mtp.agency

@mtp_agency

Milton Keynes UK
Ingram Content Group UK Ltd.
UKHW031122260824
447446UK00006B/448

9 781800 944589